ABBY'S JOURNEY

EMILY AND EMILIE III

By

David A. Margulis

Author of

The Caveman's Guide to House Repairs

Emily and Emilie

Emily and Emilie II

Dedication

This book is dedicated to my Lord and Savior Jesus Christ. Without the Lord, I would never have had the talent to write this, or anything else. I thank my wife Emily for allowing me to use her name. My son Douglas, and daughter Alexis for their names, and the full support of my wife, children, and friends for this endeavor. I also must thank Nancy Taylor (my editor) for fixing my mistakes.

Foreword

After the completion of the first book in this series, I was asked for a sequel. While working on the second book, I realized there needs to be a third. Something to tie up any loose ends that may be out there hanging around.

I welcome any comments you may have about this series. Please email me at:

Cavemansguide@hotmail.com

Chapter 1

May 27, 1989.

Abby is a shy ten-year-old girl with long dark brown hair living with her father and step mother somewhere in Florida in the United States of America. She is a quiet girl with very few friends.

Abby loves playing doctor with her dolls. She dreams of one day becoming a doctor and she even set up a little doll hospital in her parents' garage.

It's a large two car garage with a table in the back to one side. Since her parents only have one car, there is plenty of room for Abby to play.

Abby currently has the table set up as her operating table. She is stitching up the leg of a stuffed dog that tore off when she was twirling it around over her head. It's an old stuffed dog that she has had since she was three years old. As she puts in the final stitch, the leg falls off. Abby examines the patient and realizes the material is so old and worn it won't hold the stitches.

She turns to her imaginary nurse, and says. "It's a shame we couldn't save the leg."

She sews up the hole, where the leg fell off, and throws the leg towards the back wall of the garage. When she is finished with her surgery, she tells her nurse that it's a shame about the leg, but the patient will live. It's another successful operation by Dr. Abby Alexis.

She places a small blanket over the dog on the table, and tells it to rest. Abby puts the needle and thread away in their box, and goes to pick up the stuffed leg from the dog that she tossed aside. She looks all over the garage, but doesn't see the leg anywhere. Becoming frustrated because she can't find the leg, she picks up the stuffed dog, and throws it at the back wall. The dog vanishes as it passes right through the wall. Abby stands there scratching her head. Not understanding how the dog could just disappear like that. She walks up to the wall, and puts her hand on it. Her hand passes right through the wall, and she can't see it. She takes a step forward, and finds herself in a busy furniture factory.

The stuffed dog is lying at her feet, with her leg a couple of feet away. A man as old as her grandfather comes over to her, and (with a strange accent) asks her where she came from. He tells her she shouldn't be in the shop. He takes her by the hand, leads her to the factory door, and pushes her outside. He goes back inside, and Abby is now outside the shop on the pavement. People are bustling about, and the sounds of the city are quite foreign to her. Abby is surprised to see horse drawn carts and carriages going down the lane with very odd-looking cars passing them. Abby walks to the end of the street where a little girl about her age is crying. Abby asks her why she is crying, and the girl shows her a broken doll. Abby takes the doll from the girl and says, "Don't worry. Dr. Abby can fix her."

Abby looks the doll over, and has an idea of how to fix her. The problem is that all her tools are in her parent's garage. She sits on the pavement next to the girl and ponders the situation. She asks the girl if it is all right for them to take the doll into the furniture factory. The girl shrugs her shoulders, and the two of them go into the factory. Abby asks one of the men if they have a pair of pliers she can borrow. The man laughs at her and tells her to leave. Abby sees a table full of tools near the back wall. She ignores the man and goes straight to the tools to start her operation on the doll. The work in the factory stops as all the workers are watching as Abby repairs the broken doll. When she does all that she can do, she hands the doll back to the girl, and all the workmen applaud her efforts. Even the foreman applauds, then tells the men to get back to work. The little girl thanks Abby then takes her doll, and runs off down the lane. Abby starts to feel uneasy about where she is. She looks around and none of the workmen are watching her, so she goes back to the wall that she passed through (she picks up the stuffed dog) and is back in her parent's garage. Abby runs into the house to tell her stepmother about her adventure, but she is told to be quiet. Her stepmother says she is busy and for Abby to come back later. Abby walks away dejected to her room and closes the door.

At the dinner table, Abby's stepmother tells her father that she enrolled Abby in a sleep away camp for the summer. The camp starts in a few days, so they have to get her ready to go right away. He doesn't like the idea, but since the fees are already paid there isn't much he can do about it.

Abby climbs onto her bed and her dad sits next to her and tells her she will have a wonderful time at camp. (He pauses) and says he will miss her every minute she's away. She puts on a brave face, and tells him she will do her best to have fun. Before she has a chance to tell him about her adventure through the wall. The lights are out. The door is closed and she is alone. She has trouble falling asleep, so she turns on her night light, and plays with her dolls. One doll is a doctor, one is a nurse, and one is the patient. The patient has chicken pox, so Abby takes a crayon, and makes dots all over the doll. The doctor, and nurse discuss how best to treat the patient. When suddenly the bedroom door flies open. Her stepmother storms into the room grabs the dolls from Abby, and throws them into the closet.

She turns off the night light and shouts.
"Go to sleep." As Abby lays down, a tear slowly rolls down her cheek.

"I will not cry. I will not cry." She murmurs softly to herself, as she tries to fall asleep. She tosses and turns until finally she's asleep.

Early the next morning she is awakened by her stepmother yelling at Abby to get ready. She tells Abby they have to go out and get everything she needs for camp. When they arrive at the store, there is only one parking space available. They have to walk quite a distance to get to the store, and that makes her stepmother angry.

Once inside, the store is crowded with parents and children picking up everything they need for camp. Abby's stepmother walks up to a man who appears to be the manager. She whispers in his ear kisses him on the cheek and hands him the list and some cash. She stands there smiling, while Abby walks around the store. Every time she is about ten feet from her stepmother, she hears a shout and Abby comes slowly back to her. After four tries, Abby stands by her stepmother's side and waits.

After about twenty minutes, the man comes back and calls one of his associates to carry everything out to their car. Abby's stepmother gives the man a kiss and a piece of paper. She grabs Abby by the hand and practically drags her back to their car.

After the car is parked in the garage, Abby is ordered to take everything into her room, and place everything on the camp list into the footlocker that they just purchased. Abby does as she is told, and when she is finished asks if she can play with her dolls. Her stepmother is on the phone, and ignores Abby's question. Abby goes back into her room and plays with her dolls.

Abby is so excited about all the new things her stepmother purchased for her and wants to show everything to her father. After dinner, she asks him to go with her into her room so she can show him. He sits on her bed, and she pulls everything out of the footlocker to show to her dad. When she pulls out the final item, he tells her that everything is very nice and storms out of her room. He begins shouting at her stepmother for spending so much money on all new clothes when Abby could very easily have packed the clothes she already owns.

While they are shouting, Abby repacks her footlocker and closes her bedroom door. It is difficult for her to fall asleep with all the shouting, but finally Abby nods off.

The morning sun shining through her window wakes Abby up. She wanders around to find her father and stepmother, but she is alone in the house. She pours herself a bowl of cereal for breakfast and then goes into the garage to operate on another doll.

This will be a serious operation. The head, arms, and legs were all torn off by Abby's stepmother while she was shouting last night. It takes Abby most of the day to put the doll back together. When she is finished putting her doll together, the car-horn sounds from the driveway. That is her signal to open the garage door. After the car is in the garage and Abby closes the garage door, her stepmother waits in the car for Abby to get close enough so that she will be hit by the opening car-door. Abby had learned her lesson, and walks around the back of the car and up on the passenger side, making her stepmother furious.

Abby goes to her table as her stepmother slams the car-door and goes into the house without saying a word. Abby's escape is her doll hospital dream world. She prays for the day she will be old enough to move away and not have to deal with her stepmother.

Abby stands there staring at the portal wall and wonders if she should go through it again. She knows that if she does go and her stepmother calls for her she would be in trouble for not answering. All she can do is daydream and wait for the ominous shout for her to go back into the house. With nothing more to do in the garage, Abby goes inside the house and asks her stepmother if she can go in the backyard and play on the swings. Her stepmother is on the phone and just waves her arm at Abby to leave her alone. Abby takes her stuffed dog with the missing leg outside with her and swings on the swings with her.

She has been outside for quite some time when there is a shout from the back door. It is time to open the garage door so that her stepmother can go pick up her father from work. After the car pulls away, Abby closes the door and stands looking at the portal wall. It will take her stepmother about an hour to return with her father, so Abby decides to go through the portal. When she arrives in the furniture factory, there is no one around, the lights are out, and it is very dark. She doesn't understand since it was daylight when she left her garage. She spends about a half an hour looking around in the dark, and then goes back home. Once at home, she flops down on her bed and thinks about her mini adventure and the rest of her day's activities.

The next morning Abby is taken to a school parking lot to get the bus to go to camp. All the parents are waving to their children as the buses pull away. Abby's stepmother dropped her off and sped away as fast as she could, leaving Abby alone. She smiles, thinking that she will have most of the summer away from her stepmother. She misses her father, but carries a photo of him that she looks at to make her happy.

Chapter 2

August 7, 1989.

Her summer at camp flew by quickly, and Abby is nervous about returning home. She is not in the mood to be yelled at by her stepmother.

The buses drop the campers off at a local school. Everyone's parents are happy to see their campers come home. Abby looks all over for her father, but she doesn't see him anywhere. She sits on the curb, ignoring the horn honking from the other side of the parking lot. After a few minutes, her stepmother's car comes to a screeching stop towards her with her stepmother shouting at her.

"Didn't you hear me honking. What's wrong with you? Get your things, and get in the car. I don't have all day to waste on you." It takes Abby two trips to get all of her belongings into her stepmother's car. The entire time Abby is loading her things, her stepmother sits behind the wheel listening to the radio. Abby opens the passenger door and is yelled at to get in the back.

"Always in the back," she shouts at Abby.

As the car pulls into the driveway, Abby is told to go open the garage door, so her stepmother can pull the car into the garage. When the car stops, her stepmother gets out and starts towards the door into the house. As she is entering the house, she yells at Abby to close the garage door and put all her things away. Abby refuses to cry, but she so feels like it. After she is totally unpacked, she asks if she could play in the garage.

"Don't you dare touch my car," her stepmother shouts at her.

When Abby gets into the garage, she notices that everything in the garage has been rearranged and there are now two cars parked in it. Her table is gone, and the cars take up most of the free space. Abby wonders if her secret doorway is still there, but as she is about to try it her stepmother calls for her to come into the house. As soon as she enters the house, her stepmother shouts at her.

"Here is a list of chores for you to do while I go pick up your father. Make sure everything on this list is done by the time I get back." She grabs her purse from the table and shouts, "Open the garage door for me."

Abby opens the door and watches her stepmother drive away. Once the car is out of sight. Abby looks over her list of chores. "Vacuum, dust, wash the dishes in the sink, and take out the trash."

As she is taking out the trash, Abby tosses the list in the bin and slams the lid shut. She washes the dishes and runs around quickly with the vacuum. She doesn't bother dusting, but goes into her room, and starts writing in a journal that she had started in summer camp. She fills in missing stories of summer camp, and how horrible her stepmother treats her. After about fifteen minutes, a car horn is heard from the driveway. As she enters the garage, her stepmother's car is pulling in, and her father is standing by the outer door. He smiles and waves at her and she smiles and waves back. He motions for her to come to him. As she is passing the car, her stepmother opens the door quickly knocking Abby down with it.

As she gets out of the car she shouts, "You should watch where you are going."

Abby's dad saw what happened, and starts to shout at his wife. She ignores him and walks into the house. Abby runs to her father, and they hug each other. He kisses her forehead and says, "How about we go out for dinner? Just the two of us."

She smiles, and shakes her head yes. They get into his car and drive off without her stepmother.

When they get home from dinner, her parents yell and shout at each other.

Abby hides in her room and takes out her journal. After she finishes writing, she searches her room for a place to hide the journal, so her stepmother doesn't find it. Abby crawls around in her closet and finds a loose floorboard. Using a letter-opener, she pries the board up and finds an empty space with a letter in it. She puts the journal in the space and covers the opening again.

She takes the letter to her bed to read it. The envelope only has a date written on it. "1965." She opens the envelope, takes the letter out and starts to read it.

"My name is Douglas Lennon. I built this house with my own two hands. Just as I was putting the finishing touches on the garage, I noticed an unusual phenomenon. The wall seemed to be a doorway to the past. When I walked through it, I found myself in London England in the year 1885. I fell in love with the city and decided not to go back to 1965. If the doorway to the past is still working, look me up. I own and operate a pub called "The East End Pub." Enjoy your travels. Douglas Lennon." Abby folds the letter, and stuffs it back into the envelope. She takes out her journal, writes about finding the letter and her hope of one day visiting Mr. Lennon at his pub. She also writes about how horrible her stepmother treats her. Oh, how she wishes she could go through the portal and never come back just like Mr. Lennon did. She rereads that part, and it makes her smile. Abby finishes her writing and puts the envelope she found in her journal. She puts the journal in its hiding place and puts a box of dolls over it to make it harder to see.

Chapter 3

August 19, 1992.

The tension in the Alexis household is getting stronger by the day. As Abby and her stepmother are always at odds with each other. When Abby's father is home, he also argues with his wife. Abby is happy when school is in session, and she doesn't have to be home. Her father accepts a new job where he has to travel, so he is on the road most of the time. Abby doesn't bother going through the time portal as her stepmother and homework keep her very busy. Halfway through the school year, Abby comes home and her stepmother isn't home. This is very unusual because she insists on giving Abby her to-do list as soon as she comes home from school. A week passes and there is no sign or word from her stepmother. Her father seems relieved that he doesn't have to argue with her anymore. Abby becomes the mother of the house. Cooking and cleaning and taking care of everything. Her father is only home a few days a week, and the two of them seem very happy with the way things are at this time. Being so busy, Abby forgets all about the time portal, and keeps herself occupied with her schoolwork and housework. As the years pass by, they seem to be picking up momentum. In what seems like the blink of an eye, Abby is celebrating her sweet sixteen. Her father is promoted to a new position at work, so he no longer needs to travel. Abby is very happy to have him home every day. With the lack of friends and taking care of her father, Abby spends most of her time on her studies. On her seventeenth birthday, she graduates from high school and enrolls in the nursing program at a local college. The dream of becoming a doctor is still in her heart, but her finances won't allow it. She decides to become a nurse instead of a doctor and then try to become a doctor later in life.

August 16, 1997.

Abby decides it is time to clean out her closet and throw away her childhood toys. She steps on the loose board in the closet and reveals the journal with the letter she found seven years ago. She opens the letter and rereads it. Putting it down on her bed she goes to the garage to see if the portal still exists. She is very surprised to find that it works, and she finds herself back in the furniture factory. The factory is still here, but no one is around. She goes to open the door and finds that it isn't locked. She walks out onto the pavement and goes down the end of lane. The building directly adjacent to the old furniture factory is The East End Pub. She thinks about the name from the letter she found in her closet. She remembers that in the letter he said if you ever come here, to look him up. She stands up tall to make herself look older and goes into the pub. There are a dozen or more older men in the pub. All of them are looking her over and making rude remarks. The man behind the bar asks them to calm down and he beckons Abby to come to him.

"Can I help you with something young lady?" the man asks her. Abby asks the man where she can find a Douglas Lennon. The barman asks her, "Which one?"

She says she isn't sure and asks him how many Douglas Lennons are there? The barman tells her that he is Douglas Lennon and his son is also Douglas Lennon. She asks him if his son was born here or somewhere else. He tells her he was born here and points to the apartment door in the back of the pub. She pauses for a moment and tells him she is looking for who she assumes is the senior Mr. Lennon. He tells her that he is Douglas Lennon Sr. Then he inquires of her what she wants with him. She leans in close so that no one else can hear and tells him that she read his letter. He leans back and tells her he has written many letters. To which one is she referring?

Very softly she says. "The one dated 1965." Douglas' eyes and mouth open wide.

"It still works," he says. Abby smiles and says that if he means the magic wall, she is living proof. He offers her a drink but she refuses.

"I'm only eighteen." She whispers. Then she tells him she doesn't want to stay long she just wanted to say hello and tell him that she read his letter. Abby says that she does have one question though. She asks him what the year is. He softly tells her that it is 1917. He asks her if she needs to know anything else, and she asks him why the furniture factory is empty. He points to the crowd in the pub and tells her they are all in here for a break. She thanks him and tells him she has to go. He tells her to come back anytime, and the drinks would be on him. She thanks him and goes on her way.

She wanders around the streets of London for a couple of hours, then decides to go home.

After Abby is home for a few days, she goes to the library to look up "The Great War." She doesn't understand why everyone she saw in the past was talking about it. Since everyone in the past is mentioning the great war she wants to know what it was all about. The more she reads about the war the more she is convinced that she wants to become a doctor. She talks to her father about medical school; but as he has told her in the past, "We just can't afford it."

With her dream of becoming a doctor put aside, Abby dives head first into her nursing studies. In the back of her mind is always the thought of visiting the past; but being so busy with school work, taking care of the house and nursing studies, Abby just doesn't have any free time to do anything else.

June 29, 1998.

Abby is studying diseases of the respiratory system. She remembers in her reading about WWI that many people were infected with influenza. She decides to go through the portal and see the epidemic first-hand. It is about midnight London time when she exits the warehouse. She sees a Policeman and asks him where the local hospital is. He asks her if she is having a medical emergency, and she says no. She tells him that she just wants to see the hospital. He thinks that's strange, but offers to take her there as it isn't that far to walk. It is a nice evening, and they are having a pleasant conversation. At one point, the officer asks her if she is sick or visiting someone in particular. She tells him she isn't sick, she is a nursing student and is just going to the hospital to look around. Once she says that she is a nursing student, instead of leading her to the hospital, he leads her to the nurses' dormitory. He reprimands her for being out after curfew and that Sister will be very annoyed with her for being outside at this hour. Abby has no idea what he is talking about, and the only Sister she knows was a teacher of religious studies in her high school. She goes along with his directions as she figures she is on a fact-finding mission. The officer knocks on the door of the nurses' dormitory, and an older woman answers the door. The officer tells her that one of her students got lost and he is bringing her back. The woman thanks the officer and ushers Abby into the dorm. She closes and locks the door and looks deeply into Abby's eyes. The woman looks curiously at Abby and asks her who she is as she doesn't recognize Abby as one of her students. Abby, (thinking fast) tells her that she isn't from around here. She is just visiting and wants to see how their hospitals are handling the influenza outbreak. The woman introduces herself, but Abby is only half paying attention. She hears the word Sister, but doesn't catch her name. Abby's attention is drawn to the small group of girls at the top of the stairs giggling and pointing at her. Sister tells her that there is no way she is going to let Abby outside at this hour and that she would find her a bed and some decent clothes to wear for the night. Abby is wearing her favorite blue jeans and a t-shirt. She didn't think about how the clothing in 1918 was so much different than the clothing in 1998. Sister calls up to the group of girls for Hyacinth to come down. One of the girls comes slowly down the stairs. Sister just shoots a look at the group and they all scatter to their rooms. Hyacinth is a short thin redhaired girl. When she comes to the bottom of the stairs, she asks Sister what she had done wrong.

Sister says, "Nothing child. This young lady needs a bed for the night, and you have a spare bed in your room."

Abby can see the relief on the girl's face as she begins to smile, "Find her some decent bed clothes also," Sister calls out as Hyacinth takes Abby by the hand and leads her up the stairs.

Once they are in the bedroom, Hyacinth closes the door. Abby introduces herself as does Hyacinth. Hyacinth points to a bed and tells Abby that she can have that one. Hyacinth says she would find Abby a nightdress and she leaves the room. Hyacinth comes back about ten minutes later with a small pile of clothes. She hands the clothes to Abby and sits on her bed watching Abby get undressed.

"Is there a problem?" Abby asks.

"I've never seen a girl wearing trousers before." Hyacinth replies.

Abby isn't sure what to say so she just says, "Thank you for the clothes and good night."

Abby is awakened by Hyacinth shoving her and telling her to wake up. "It's late; we'll miss breakfast." Hyacinth says, as Abby slowly gets herself upright and out of bed. Abby takes off the nightgown and doesn't notice Hyacinth sitting watching her. She looks at the pile of clothes and has no idea how to put them on. She turns to call for help and sees Hyacinth sitting there watching her. "Could you please help me get dressed?" Abby asks her. Hyacinth smiles and says. "Yes."

After she is fully clothed Abby turns to Hyacinth and tells her where she is from they don't were anything like this. Hyacinth just smiles, and lets out a little laugh.

"Not much for conversation." Abby thinks.

They run downstairs to the main dining hall and join the rest of the girls at the table. Sister turns to Abby and tells her she looks much more appropriate this morning. Abby thanks her for everything, eats as fast as she can and leaves to go home. She never did make it to the hospital. When she gets into her house, her father sees her in her 1918 student nurse's uniform.

"Don't tell me you have to wear that?" Her father says.

She tells him she just wanted to get a feel for how nurses worked in the past.

He says. "Thank God for that. I couldn't imagine working in that get-up all day." Abby glares at him and as sharp as she has ever spoken to him says. "Men are lucky, they never did."

He is surprised by her tone, but says nothing more about it. Abby goes to her room to change her clothes and puts her new outfit carefully on a hanger in her closet.

When she takes out her journal to write about her night in 1918, she writes about how time runs different in 1998 than it does in 1918. She writes that she left her home at seven in the evening and arrived in the furniture factory at midnight. Spent the entire night in 1918 and got home about a half an hour after she had left. Her conclusion is that one hour in the past is equal to one minute in the present. "As of this writing." She added.

A week later, Abby takes the uniform out and heads to the hospital in 1918. This time she makes sure to leave at a time that would put her in the past at a decent hour. Not at midnight. She walks into the hospital and no one questions her. Being dressed as a nurse everyone who sees her assumes she works there. Abby wanders around the hospital for a couple of hours and then leaves. Most of the hospital is filled with either young men she assumes are wounded from the war or people suffering from influenza. She has a small notebook with her and is taking notes about what she sees.

Back at home she is lighter than air. Feeling wonderful, she pulls out her journal and (using her notes) writes all about her day wandering the halls of the hospital in 1918.

Chapter 4

June 16, 2001.

Abby's graduation party is a small affair. Just herself and her father. She never took the time to make friends in school as she devoted all her time to her studies. She graduated first in her class and was offered a position in the hospital associated with the University she attended. With only a week before work starts, Abby decides to enjoy her week of freedom. She goes to visit Douglas Lennon to say hello. She puts on her 1918 nurse's uniform and goes through the portal. When she gets into the furniture factory, the entire building is vacant. Now it looks like an empty warehouse. Abby goes to The East End to see Douglas Lennon, and he is happy to see her again. He asks her why she took so long to return and if she is old enough to drink. Abby (says with a laugh) she is old enough and would he be so kind as to pour her an ale. He smiles pours her a drink, and he asks her again why she hasn't been back to visit him in such a long time. Abby is confused and asks him what the year is. Douglas tells her it is 1931. Abby is confused by his response. She thought it would be 1921. While trying to figure out where ten years disappeared, a young lady breezes past them, and Douglas tries to get her attention. She shouts out. "Later. I'm late." And she is gone.

Douglas tells Abby that is his daughter Emilie. Abby and Emilie, seem to be about the same age, and Abby says it would be nice if they could meet one day. Abby is all for meeting her, but for the moment is happy telling Douglas all about how things have changed since he left in 1965. After filling him in on the latest advances in the world of the future, she asks him if he understands that she was here three years ago, and it was 1918 and now it is 1931. He looks curiously at her and tells her he has no idea what she is talking about.

Abby notices the time on the clock on the wall and tells Douglas that she has to leave. He asks her where she is off to, and she says, "The hospital." She thanks him for the drink and he tells her to come back soon.

She leaves the pub and strolls casually to the hospital. It is the 1930s, and people are in very sad shape. The Great War is over, the influenza epidemic has passed, and for ten short years everyone was in better spirits.

Then the Great Depression hit, and the economies of the world have been devastated. When Abby walks into the hospital, no one questions her. Everyone just assumes she is a nurse there, and says hello as they pass her in the halls. She wanders the halls, and stops in a patient's room every now and then to reads a chart to see how things are done.

On this particular day, she is reading a chart, and a doctor comes into the room. He clears his throat to get her attention. He extends his hand and asks her for the chart. She is concerned because there is an error in the medication. She doesn't know if she should mention it to him or not. Abby waits for the doctor to finish reading the chart and examine the patient. After his examination, he says, "Very good." And turns to leave the room. Abby puts her hand on his shoulder and the doctor becomes indignant. "How dare you touch me." He shouts at her.

This angers Abby. Not only is he prescribing the wrong medication, but he has a terrible attitude as well. Abby stares him straight in the eyes, and tells him they must speak about this patient. As he is about to walk away from her, Matron comes walking down the hallway. Abby does her best to avoid Matron as she can get Abby into serious trouble. Matron walks up to the doctor and asks him if there is a problem. He says there most definitely is. She had better train her nurses to respect him better. That is all Abby needs to hear. In her mind she says. "The gloves are off."

Matron turns to Abby and asks for her name.

Abby hesitantly says, "Abigail Alexis." After hearing her name, Matron's facial expression changes, but Abby doesn't notice. She continues; "this doctor is prescribing the wrong medication for this patient."

Although they are in the hallway, the patient can hear their entire conversation.

"Get in here this instant." The patient calls out. Matron, the doctor and Abby go into the patient's room. The patient turns to Abby and asks her if she knows who he is. Abby is angry and ready for a fight. She blurts out without thinking.

"Someone in need of proper medical care." Matron's eyes go wide.

The doctor shouts. "What?"

The patient smiles and says, "The young lady has a point."

"She will be reprimanded immediately." Matron tells the patient.

"Nonsense," the patient says. He beckons Abby to come closer to him and asks her what is wrong with his treatment. The doctor is about to say something when the patient holds up a finger to quiet him. Abby picks up the chart and explains what the patient is suffering from. She goes on to explain the proper treatment for such an ailment.

The doctor is about to storm out of the room when Matron asks to see the chart. The doctor freezes in his tracks as Abby hands the chart to her. Matron agrees with Abby, and the doctor storms out of the room mumbling.

Matron tells the patient that another doctor will be seeing him from now on. Abby is almost certain that Matron is smiling at her, but that isn't in her nature. Matron tells Abby to meet her in her office immediately.

As Matron walks out of the room the patient reaches out and grabs Abby by the arm. He tells her that in the drawer of the table beside his bed is a stack of business cards. He tells her to take a card and call him if she ever needs his help. He thanks Abby for her diligence in standing up to the doctor and tells her she should consider being a doctor and not a nurse. Abby thanks him and reads the card as she slowly walks to Matron's office. The card read. "Dr. Bryon Jones. Chief Counselor London Medical College."

Abby smiles all the way to Matron's office. Once inside the office, Matron asks her to close the door and sit down. Matron leans towards Abby and tells her that she knows Abby doesn't work in this hospital for one reason it is her job to know every nurse on staff, and Abigail Alexis isn't one of them. For the second reason, no one wears those old uniforms anymore. Matron tells Abby that Dr. Jones is a very important man, and she may have very well saved his life.

There is a long silence, then Matron leans back in her chair and orders Abby to tell her the truth or she will have her brought up on charges. Abby sits up straight in her chair and tells Matron that she's a registered nurse from a different hospital. She tells her that she has heard many good things about this hospital, and she wanted to see for herself to see if it would be worth changing to this location from where she currently works. Matron writes down her name on a letterhead paper; and with a smile, tells Abby that this hospital would be honored to have her. "Whenever you are ready to come to us, Miss Abigail Alexis, we will be happy to have you," Matron says as she stands and shakes Abby's hand. Abby stands and thanks her.

Matron looks deep into Abby's eyes and adds, "When you are ready to tell me the real truth, I am here to listen." Abby nervously walks out and walks back to the portal as fast as she can.

June 16, 2001

Pulling out her journal, Abby writes down the entire episode. She is smiling the entire time.

After she finishes writing in her journal, Abby gets ready for work. She checks herself in the mirror and leaves for the hospital still smiling.

That evening a young couple is brought in to the maternity ward. The woman is in advanced labor with twins. Abby recognizes the couple from church. They are a nice friendly couple, and he is one of the only people who always says hello to her and asks how she is doing. He smiles at her when she walks into the room. Suddenly, the couple is at ease knowing that someone they know is there to help them. He says hello and asks her how she is doing. She smiles and says that she should be asking him that. She picks up the chart to check the details.

"Mrs. Ivanovitch?" Abby asks.

Emily says "yes."

Abby says she is just checking to make sure. She turns to the husband and says. "Your name is Dave, right?" He says yes as he sits in the corner out of the way.

By the time the second baby is delivered, Abby is at the end of her shift. She makes a point to stay a little late to make sure that Mr. and Mrs. Ivanovitch are doing well. After she checks one last time, she leaves for home. She doesn't go through the portal this time because she is too tired. She has a funny feeling about Emily Ivanovitch. It is as if she knows her from somewhere, but can't place where. When she is getting into bed, she picks up her father's picture to kiss it goodnight. Her eyes open wide as she sees the reflection of her face in the picture and realizes that Emily Ivanovitch looks exactly like her. When Abby gets to the ward the following night, Emily and Dave are already gone. She was hoping to see them and ask some questions about where Emily is from. "Hopefully at church," Abby says, as she continues with her shift.

Chapter 5

June 25, 2006.

Abby celebrates her fifth-year anniversary at the hospital. She loves working as a nurse and is truly happy working in this hospital. Currently, she is working in Maternity and is so happy to see new life coming into the world. She is on the night shift, and it is a very quiet night. Only one mother and her new daughter. Most of the staff are talking about their favorite television shows. Abby has never had any interest in television, so hers collects dust in the corner of the room. There's a TV in the sitting room that her father watches from time to time, but that one is getting its own dust collection.

Abby checks on the mother and the child, and all is well. She goes down to the cafeteria for a coffee and a snack. A co-worker runs up to her and asks her if she knows a Daniel Alexis. She says that's her father's name. The co-worker tells her to go to the ER right away. Two people are being wheeled in, a man and a woman. Abby runs up to the man, and sees that it's her father. One of the doctors asks her to step aside, and a curtain is closed in her face. Her co-worker puts her arm around her and guides her to a chair.

They sit together and wait to see, or hear, any news. The curtain shielding the woman that was brought in is opened, and the hospital staff all walk out with their eyes towards the floor. Abby goes over to see who it is. There is a sheet covering the woman, and Abby uncovers the woman's face. Abby gasps when she sees that it's her stepmother. Although sad at the loss of a life, Abby is almost happy that it was her stepmother. Abby draws the sheet back over her face and two police officers approach her. One of the officers asks her if she knows the man and woman who were brought in. Abby says she does; the woman is her stepmother, but she hasn't seen her in years. The man is her father. The policemen say they are sorry and ask if Abby wants to know what happened. She tells them she would very much like to know. The three of them sit down near her father. One of the officers takes out a small notebook and begins to tell her the information they have as of this point in time.

"The male had just been seen getting into an automobile, when another vehicle at a high rate of speed came crashing into it, striking the vehicle on the driver's side. The impact of the crash sent the female occupant flying out of her vehicle and landing on the pavement on the passenger side of his car. A bystander ran into a nearby liquor store and called the police."

The officer pauses and looks at Abby who is getting uneasy. He asks her if she wants him to continue and Abby says yes. The officer tells Abby that they found a note in the woman's purse. The note says that "Daniel Alexis ruined her life and now she is going to ruin his." At that moment, a doctor comes from behind the curtain where her father is. He sees Abby and knows her from their working together in the past. The doctor walks up to Abby and says he is sorry, that they did everything they could, but the injuries were much worse than they originally presumed. Again, he says he is sorry and slowly walks away. The officers put their hands on her shoulders and also say they are sorry. One of them says that if she needs them for anything, she can call the station. The officer with the note pad writes their names and badge numbers down and hands the note to Abby. One of the officers asks her if she needs a ride home or anything. Abby declines, saying she needs to finish her shift.

News in the hospital travels fast; and by the time Abby makes it back to maternity, they are all waiting for her and telling her how sorry they are. The shift supervisor calls Abby into her office and tells her to go home. Abby insists on staying, and a small battle of wills takes place for a few minutes. The supervisor backs down, and Abby stays for the rest of her shift.

When Abby gets home, she doesn't feel like being in the house so she goes through the portal to 1936. As she is walking towards the hospital, she sees a small girl playing with a broken doll. Abby walks up to the girl and tells her that she is "Dr. Abby the doll doctor." The little girl says her name is Carol and asks Abby if she could really fix her doll. Abby puts her hand out and takes the doll. She looks the doll over and tells the girl she can definitely fix her. Abby sits on the pavement next to the girl and opens her purse. She turns to Carol and tells her to always be prepared. Abby pulls some tools out of her purse and goes to work on the doll. After about half an hour, the doll is good as new.

Abby hands the doll back to Carol and says, "It was another successful operation by Dr. Abby the doll doctor."

Carol gives Abby a big hug and scoots off down the lane. Abby sits on the pavement feeling good about what she has just accomplished and smiles. She hasn't repaired a doll in years and is very happy with herself. A police officer comes walking up to her and asks her if she is all right. Abby tells him she is fine and sticks out her hand for him to help her up. He helps her to her feet and asks her if she is just going on, or just getting off? Abby thinks for a moment, and says. "A little of both."

Upon arriving at the hospital, Abby goes straight to Matron's office and sits down waiting for her to return. About twenty-five minutes later, Abby hears Matron's voice in the hallway. Abby stands to show the proper respect as Matron walks into the office and closes the door. Matron looks Abby over without saying a word, then tells her all the things that are wrong with the way she is dressed. After being berated by Matron, Abby forgets why she wanted to speak with her. Abby is told to exit the office, and only to return when her uniform is modern and up to standards. Abby doesn't wander the halls as she usually does. She just walks outside and wanders around the neighborhood for a couple of hours. She is hoping that she would see something that would jog her memory.

She pauses in front of a toy store and looks at the dolls in the window. Then it occurs to her what she wanted to discuss with Matron. "A doll hospital," she says out loud. The owner of the toy store is sweeping the pavement and overhears Abby's exclamation.

"There aren't any around here," the man says to her.

"There aren't any what?" Abby asks the man.

"Doll hospitals. There aren't any around here." The man answers back. Abby tells the man that she would like to open one, if she could find the right location. The man invites Abby into the shop and shows her all the dolls that he has on display. He tells her that he is in the business of selling new dolls not fixing old ones. He asks her how could he stay in business if everyone fixed their old toys instead of buying new ones. Abby is trying to come up with a rebuttal when she sees a workbench in the back. She asks the man what the workbench is for, and he tells her, "to repair broken toys." Abby smiles and asks the man if Dr. Abby could repair dolls in his shop. He helps a couple of customers while Abby waits for his reply. After the customers leave the shop, he leans on the counter and asks her, "Wouldn't you be better off sticking to healing people?"

Abby leans on the counter with her face directly in front of his and says. "I will be."

Flustered, the man turns and faces away from her. He tells her it would never work because he can't afford to pay her.

"You won't have to." Abby says, as she puts out her hand to shake on their agreement. He shakes her hand and tells her it would be on a trial basis to see how well it works.

Abby turns facing the door and smiles. Then she tells the man she will be back one day next week to work on her patients. She skips off down the street feeling as if she just won the lottery.

When she returns to her home, there are messages on her machine with condolences. She is feeling so good that she totally forgot about her father and stepmother passing. She listens to the messages and writes down the names of the people who called. Exhausted from her high, and then low feelings, Abby goes to bed.

Chapter 6

July 1, 2006.

After the funerals, Abby holds a small luncheon for her friends and co-workers. The doctor that attended to her father and her supervisor sit with Abby, and everyone else is at separate tables. There are only about a dozen people, and Abby is trying her best to put on a brave face.

After the lunch is over and everyone is leaving, the doctor hands a note to Abby. Without looking at it, she places the note in her purse to look at later. Her supervisor tells her to take the rest of the week off. With a smile, she tells Abby "that is an order, not a request."

Abby thanks the two of them and looks around. Everyone else has already left, leaving Abby alone. She pays the bill, and drives slowly home.

Once she is home, she sits on her father's chair and picks up a photo album. She has never looked at the photo albums before. It wasn't that she didn't want to, it's just that she was always busy and never got around to it.

Turning the pages, but not really looking at the pictures, she suddenly stops turning pages and is struck by a particular picture. This is the only picture that has anything written on it.

June 13, 1979. Is printed across the bottom of the picture. Abby smiles a little smile and says out loud. "Happy birthday Emilee Abigail Alexis." Abby doesn't remember ever seeing a picture of her mother, and here she is right after giving birth. Abby stares at her mother's face and can hardly believe it. She looks just like her mother, and her mother looks so very familiar. She is certain that she has seen her someplace recently.

Abby gently takes the picture out of the album and opens her purse to put it in her wallet. She sees the note from the doctor and unfolds it. The note has his name, phone number and a short message stating that if she wants to join him for dinner sometime to give him a call. She puts the note on the coffee table and continues looking at the photo album.

After she looks at the last of the pictures in the album, she puts the album on top of the doctors note. She sits staring at the blank TV screen and thinks about her father. A man she has known her entire life, and yet she knew nothing about the man. She glances over at the table next to her and notices a recessed drawer that she never noticed before. She tugs on the drawer and it doesn't budge. It is either locked or stuck, but the drawer will not open. She gets down on her knees to get a better look at the drawer and sees a lock off to the side. She spends the next two hours looking through her father's things for the key. She finds it buried in his dresser under his socks on the keyring with his spare car keys. Once she opens the lock, she tugs on the drawer. It is heavy and full of papers. She is having a hard time getting the drawer to come out. She braces herself and gives it a big tug. The drawer comes flying out causing her to flip over backwards, and the papers go flying all over the room. Abby starts to laugh and says to herself, "Must add clean up papers to my chores for today."

On her hands and knees, she starts to pick up the papers and piles them onto the coffee table. Suddenly one paper catches her attention. It looks like an official document. Abby props herself against the sofa and looks over the document. It is an authorized and notarized letter from her Grandfather giving his permission for his fourteen-year old daughter to marry a Mr. Daniel Alexis. She drops the document, and takes out the picture from her purse. She knew her mother was young when she had her, but she didn't realize how young she was. In this picture her mother was only fifteen years old. She sits staring at the picture and realizes she has no real memories of her mother. She goes through the paper pile trying to find anything else about her mother; but aside from a marriage license, there is nothing else. She sits back down on her father's chair and looks at the picture. On top of the TV is a picture of her stepmother that Abby never liked looking at. She takes the picture out of the frame, and tears it up. Then she replaces it with her mother's picture. She places it on the TV and says to the picture, "Where are you, and what happened to you?"

It was nearing eight o'clock and Abby realizes she hasn't had her dinner yet. Not in the mood to cook, she walks down the block to get a pizza. As she is waiting for her pie to cook, she notices the doctor that gave her the note sitting in the corner being very friendly with one of her co-workers. Abby keeps her back to them, so they don't see her. When her pie is ready, she walks out with her back towards the doctor and co-worker.

After she finishes her dinner, Abby takes his note and throws it away. She spends the rest of her evening staring at the picture of her mother and racking her brain to try and remember why she looks so familiar. Sometime around midnight, Abby takes the picture, and goes to her bedroom. She places the picture on her night stand and goes to sleep.

Early the next morning Abby is awakened by a sound coming from outside her back door. She takes a knife from the kitchen and peers through the back-door curtains. A man who has the appearance of a homeless person is curling up on her back porch. Abby shouts that she is armed and for the man to leave. He tells her that he is homeless and all he needs is a place to sleep for a few hours. He promises her that he will be gone by the time she comes home from work.

Abby takes the left-over pizza from last night and hands it to the man through the window. He thanks her and wishes God's blessings upon her. He eats one slice of the pizza and puts the rest away for later. Abby makes sure the house is locked and goes to take a shower.

While she is eating her breakfast, she hears the homeless man get up and leave her back porch. Abby wonders why he chose her back porch to sleep; but being a nurse, she has compassion for the man. After cleaning up from breakfast, Abby sits on her father's chair and thinks about what she wants to do today. She looks up to the ceiling and smiles. She decides to go through the portal and spend some time in 1936.

She goes to The East End to say hello to Douglas Lennon. He is happy to see her, and they have a long talk about her life and how she doesn't know what she is going to do now that her father has passed away. Douglas asks her how she is set financially and she tells him that isn't a problem. Her father had a life insurance policy that will pay all her bills. Douglas tells her he didn't mean there; he means here. She tells him she has very little 1930s money and no idea when she will earn any. Douglas smiles and whispers to her, to go back home and look up the horse racing results for later in the day. She isn't sure what he has in mind, but follows his instructions.

She goes back home and returns a few hours later. She shows the results to Douglas and he explains to her that it is too late. The racing is finished for the day. He tells her to go back home and get the results for tomorrow, and then come back early in the morning. He shows her his watch so she can understand the time difference. She agrees to return tomorrow and spends the rest of the day wandering around London.

When she is tired of walking, she goes back to the warehouse and returns home.

Abby calculates the time she needs to leave her home and works out when she needs to go to bed to get enough sleep so she can be at The East End at eight o'clock in the morning. She has to leave her house at three o'clock in the morning her time.

Abby goes to the library to look up the racing results, and then she stops at a sandwich shop for a quick bite to eat.

On her way back to her car, she is accosted by two homeless men. They are forcing her to give them her food and money. She is very afraid and about to scream when the homeless man she gave the pizza to comes to her rescue. He yells at the other homeless men and gives them each a slice of his pizza. Abby thanks him and he thanks her for her kindness.

As quickly as she could, she gets into her car and heads home. By the time she does a few chores and finishes her sandwich, it is time for her to go to bed.

Abby oversleeps and is having a hard time getting herself motivated. By the time she goes through the portal, it is four-thirty in the morning her time. She arrives at the pub a little after nine-thirty in the morning. Douglas is happy she made it on time. Abby laughs, and thinks to herself that she thought she was late. Douglas leads the way as they take the bus to the race track. When they arrive at the track, Douglas tells her to keep her notes hidden in her purse. Abby takes the paper out and shows it to Douglas. It is nothing but two columns of numbers and nothing else. She whispers to him that the first column was the winning horse and the second column was the race. They are not in order; so if anyone else looks at it, they won't know what it means. Douglas tells her that she has a devious streak in her. She smiles and says she learned it from a movie.

By the time the last race ends, they each made about two hundred pounds.

When they get back to the pub, Abby does the math and tells Douglas that the money they each made was the equivalent of about ten-thousand pounds in her money in the future.

Douglas smiles and says, "How do you think I was able to buy this pub."

Abby quietly asks him about his accent. She is curious that he sounds like he is from East London and not America. He says as the years went by he picked up the accent and never thinks about being American. As far as he is concerned, he is a Londoner. They share a couple of drinks together, and as the pub starts to get busy, Abby says goodbye and wanders down the lane.

After visiting a few different shops, Abby comes across a uniform shop where she purchases herself a new nurse's uniform.

She is so excited about her purchase she can't wait to try it on and visit a local hospital. As she wanders along the rows of stores, she is trying to figure out where she can go to change her clothes. She stops to look in the window of a toy store when she hears someone call out her name. She is a bit surprised because she doesn't remember telling anyone her name. By the time she turns around, she is face to face with Hyacinth. Hyacinth grabs her and gives her a big hug.

"I knew that was you as soon as I saw you." Hyacinth exclaims. She is bubbly and talkative. Not the shy quiet girl Abby met seven years ago. Hyacinth is asking questions non-stop not waiting for any answers, but just asking and asking more and more questions. Before Abby has a chance to say anything. Hyacinth asks her if she wants to come to her place for a cup of tea. Abby smiles but before she can say yes, Hyacinth grabs her by the hand and leads her to the nurses' housing where she is living. Hyacinth shows Abby into her room then goes to get them each a cup of tea. While she is away, Abby changes her clothes and is now ready to visit the hospital.

When Hyacinth returns with the tea, she is surprised to see Abby in her uniform. She has a couple of things out of place, and Hyacinth shows her the correct way to wear her uniform. They finish their tea, and Hyacinth takes her on a tour of the hospital. As they are finishing their tour, Abby sees Matron in her office. She looks carefully so Matron won't see her. Suddenly, Abby's face lights up. She now knows why the picture of her mother looks so familiar. She looks just like Matron. Or does it? Matron looks just like her mother. Abby wants to run to her and tell her who she is, but Hyacinth tugs her away. Hyacinth tells Abby that she isn't in Matron's good graces because of a mistake she made the previous day. She rushes Abby out of the hospital and back to her room. Hyacinth keeps talking as Abby changes her clothes. As she gets ready to leave, Hyacinth gives Abby her telephone number and tells her that she must keep in touch. Abby says she will and leaves the nurses' housing, making her way back to the portal. When she gets back home, she hangs up her new uniform next to the older one. She stands and stares at them for a good five minutes before she closes the closet door. After going into the sitting-room she sits on her father's chair. Although it is only about one in the afternoon, Abby is tired, and dozes off for a nap.

Chapter 7

July 10, 2006.

The entire time that Abby was away from her job she was hopping back and forth between the 1930s and the present. She went to the race track a few more times and amassed quite a large sum of money. By the time her week away from work was over, she had over two thousand 1930s pounds. A modern value of close to One-hundred thousand pounds. Abby does the math over and over and smiles. "I'm rich," she says to her pile of pound notes.

Once a week, Abby goes to the toy store and puts on her Dr. Abby persona. She is getting busier every week, and the store owner is happily surprised by the amount of money he is making from Abby repairing old broken dolls. When she finishes her last patient, the man gives her a cup of tea and an envelope. He tells her how happy he is with the work she has been doing and his business has grown because of her. When she finishes her tea, she puts the envelope into her purse and gets up to leave. He looks at her and simply says, "Open it."

She puts her purse down and takes out the envelope. There is a letter surrounding two one-pound notes.

The letter says, "Thank you for all you do. This is a small gift to show you my appreciation." Abby places the money on the counter and tells him that they agreed she would not be paid. He tells her this isn't payment just a thank you gift. He also says he will not accept it back. It's hers to do with as she pleases. She gives him a big hug and brings the money to the soup kitchen at the end of the road. The Vicar is so happy he can hardly contain himself. He must have said thank you fifty times, and Abby later wrote all about it in her journal.

After her week away, she starts back to work at the hospital on the night shift. She enjoys working nights because it is quieter and there are less distractions than day shifts. When she gets home from work she goes through the portal and visits the 1930s for a few hours. She does this for the next three years. Every now and then she stops and looks at Matron, but she never has the nerve to speak to her.

Abby enjoys hopping back to the 1930s and is learning so much more about medicine than she is in the present. Without all the modern technology, everything is more personal and hands on in the 1930s.

April, 2009.

Sunday at church Dave greets Abby and introduces her to his children as Aunt Abby. He tells her that if she ever needs anything to let him know. He is quite handy and tries to help anyone in the church who needs him. After the service, as they are walking to their cars, Abby asks Dave if he has some time to chat over a cup of coffee. There is something she wants to discuss with him. He checks with Emily, and she says it's fine with her. Later that week, they meet at the coffee shop and Abby asks him if he would be willing to help her clear out all her father's old things and take them to the thrift shop. He tells her he is free on the weekend and would be glad to help her.

Saturday April 24, 2009.

Dave arrives at Abby's house at nine-thirty in the morning. He knocks on the door, but receives no answer. Abby had come back late from her jaunt to the 1930s and was sound asleep. Dave knocks for about five more minutes with no answer. As he is walking to his car, Abby comes to the door in her pajamas. Still half asleep, she calls out to Dave. He turns and sees her in the doorway looking like she just woke up. He asks her if she wants him to come back another time, but she says no and invites him inside. Abby asks Dave to sit at the kitchen table while she changes and gets herself presentable.

He sees the coffee maker on the counter and begins the process of making coffee for the two of them. By the time she comes back to the kitchen, the coffee is ready and they both sit down and enjoy a cup. When the cups are empty, they go into her father's room and start to put her father's things into large plastic bags.

When they are finished, there are six bags full to overflowing with mostly clothing, but there are also some items that Abby no longer wants. They put the bags into his car and together they drive to the thrift shop. As they pull into the parking lot, the homeless man that Abby gave the pizza to is sitting near the dumpster. Abby says hello to him and rummages through one of the bags. She pulls out some clothes and gives them to the man. He stands up and smiles at her. As he puts his arms out to receive the clothes, he says, "My name is John. Just in case you wanted to know."

She tells him her name is Abby and thanks him for helping her at the sandwich shop. Abby is feeling good about helping him, and they chat for a few minutes. When she makes it back to Dave, the car is unloaded and he is ready to leave. She waves to John as she and Dave drive away and is pleased with herself for the good deed she did for him. She asks Dave how his wife and twin boys are doing, and he says they are all fine.

He pulls the car into her driveway, and she asks him in for another cup of coffee. He declines, saying he really needs to be getting home. They share their goodbye and expectations to see each other in church and he is gone.

Chapter 8

June 6, 2010.

Dave greets Abby at church, and she asks him if he is free the following weekend to help her again. He tells her that he will call her in the middle of the week if he is going to be free on the weekend. On Wednesday Dave calls Abby to confirm that he will be able to help her on Saturday.

He arrives at her house Saturday morning with two cups of coffee. Just as he is about to knock on the door, the door flies open and Abby greets him with a smile. Dave hands her one of the cups of coffee and says good morning. Abby thanks him for the coffee and leads him into the house.

They sit at the table for a few minutes sipping their coffee and chatting about church and the current political climate. When their coffee cups are about half empty, Abby begins to explain why she needs his help. She tells him that she went to store some things up in the attic and found a dozen or more boxes up there. She has no idea what they are and needs help bringing them down and putting them in the garage so she can go through them. Abby shows him where the attic stairs are and pulls the rope to lower them. The boxes are all lined up neatly against one side of the attic, about ten feet from the stairs opening.

Abby goes into the attic and pushes the boxes one by one towards the opening. Dave then takes the boxes and carries them down the stairs and lines them up neatly in the garage. When Dave places the fourteenth and final box in the garage, the box tips over and some of the contents spill out. As he tries to prevent further spillage, a small cassette tape recorder slides out of the box and goes right through the time portal. Abby enters the garage and finds Dave about to put his hand through the portal.

"Wait!" She shouts out surprising Dave and causing him to stop moving. Abby has a shocked expression on her face as Dave looks at her to see why she shouted at him. She tells him not to touch the wall as he tries to explain to her that a tape recorder just vanished in front of his eyes. Abby wasn't thinking about the portal when she told Dave to stack the boxes in the garage. He had placed them all where the portal is. Abby walks over to Dave and reaches out her hand to help him up. He is looking quite confused, and Abby hoping she can trust him with her little secret, asks him to go back into the house and she will explain the disappearing tape recorder to him. They sit back down at the kitchen table and Abby begins to explain to him her story. She can tell he isn't believing her tale of traveling through the portal into the past, so she gets up and gets the picture of her mother from her room. She shows him the picture, and he asks her how she got a picture of his Emily, and who is Emilee?

She tells him that she is Emilee and that is not his wife in the picture, but her mother. He sits there just staring at the picture. He can't believe the resemblance between her mother and his wife. He asks her for more pictures of her mother, but she says this is the only picture she has. He starts to look back and forth between the picture and Abby. He says that he never noticed before how much she and his wife Emily look so much alike. Abby says that she doesn't think so, and gets up to make more coffee.

Dave sits there not saying a word, but just looking deep into the face of Abby's mother's picture. When Abby returns to the table with the refilled cups, Dave asks her. "So, when are you going to explain the disappearing tape recorder?"

Abby sits back and holds her cup with both hands looking up to the ceiling. She leans forward and smiles. Then she says that she wants to tell him something that he won't believe. But before she does he must promise on her Bible that he will never tell a single person what she is about to reveal to him. Dave promises, and Abby begins her tale about the portal and Douglas. She even tells him about going to the hospital and Dr. Jones. When she is finished she asks him what he thinks about the story she just told him. He smiles and asks her what channel she saw this on and is it available on video? Abby leans further towards him and tells him she can prove it. But again, she says he must promise to never tell a soul. He promises, and she stands up.

"Follow me." She says as she walks towards the garage. When he steps into the garage, Dave asks her if they are in the past yet or still in the present.

Abby smiles, and says, "Follow me."

She then walks through the wall where he had placed all the boxes. He is a little hesitant, but shouts, "Geronimo!" and walks through the wall.

When he gets into the warehouse, Abby is smiling at him holding the tape recorder. "Recognize this?" She asks.

Dave is a little stunned, but feels as long as Abby is here with him, everything she said must be the truth. She goes on to explain that they are in London England in the year 1930. The great depression is starting and they need to be careful how they interact with the locals. She asks him if he is ready.

He shakes his head and smiles. They walk out of the warehouse and onto the pavement. Instead of walking towards the East End Pub, she takes him in the opposite direction. She isn't ready to introduce him to Douglas, so she takes him as far away from the pub as she can. After wandering the streets for about an hour and a half, Dave looks at his watch. The hands aren't moving, and he thinks the battery must be dead. He tells Abby that it must be getting late, and that he needs to get back home. Abby smiles and lets out a little laugh. They walk for another half an hour, and end up back at the warehouse.

Once back inside Abby's garage, Dave looks at his watch and the hands are moving. He asks her if she ever noticed that problem before, and she tells him she never noticed. The only thing that she says that is really odd is that time in the past is different than in the present. He doesn't understand what she means, and she tells him that one hour in the past is only about one minute in their present. The years seem to move at the same pace; and when she is in the present and goes back, the same amount of time has passed. "Sometimes though," she says "the years become jumbled. As if time passes more slowly. I can't explain it, but at one point I thought three years passed but in reality ten years had passed."

Dave is confused, and Abby tells him that if he goes through the portal in one week it would be one week later in the past.

Dave thanks her for the trip to 1930, and Abby begs him not to say anything to anyone. He promises he will never mention it to anyone ever. Abby gives him a hug and thanks him for helping her and understanding her little secret. He says good bye and drives off.

Abby goes into the garage and moves all the boxes to the opposite wall. She becomes too tired to look through them and goes inside to rest.

For the next few weeks, Abby forgets all about the boxes, and concentrates on her work and visiting the hospital in 1930.

September 7, 2010.

Abby finishes work at seven in the morning. Driving home, she realizes it's been some time since she has been to the hospital in 1930. She misses going there and is really in the mood to go.

By the time she makes it home it is almost eight o'clock. She sits at her table and works out a time chart to make sure she would be back home in time to go to work. As she is writing, she remembers that an hour in the past is equal to about a minute in the present. So therefore, a ten-hour shift in 1930 would really only take her ten minutes in present time. She stops and thinks some more about it. She writes down that if one week passes in both realities how can one hour be one minute. Then it occurs to her that the slowness of time is only when she is in the past not when she is in the present. She postulates that her being in the past is what is slowing down the present.

Abby makes a quick cup of coffee and changes her clothes.

When she goes through the portal it is two thirty in the afternoon in London. She takes a brisk walk to the hospital and starts her usual routine of walking into rooms and reading charts. She enjoys talking to the patients about their families and their life. The patients respond well to her and most of them are smiling when she leaves their rooms.

With the exception of a few, they tell her that they look forward to seeing her again. As she is leaving the room of a Mr. Hopkirk, Abby walks right into Matron. Matron smiles, and tells Abby that she hasn't seen her in a while. She asks Abby to follow her to her office, as they need to have a little talk. While turning a corner, Matron is face to face with Mr. Bronson, the chief surgeon. He starts to shout at her the instant he sees her. It seems they are short staffed, and Mr. Bronson has to perform emergency surgery and has no operating room nurse to assist him. He shouts at Matron that if she doesn't supply a nurse immediately he will force her to assist him.

Matron grabs Abby by the arm and pulls her towards Mr. Bronson.

"Here is your assistant Mr. Bronson," Matron says, as she shoves Abby into him. Mr. Bronson grabs Abby by the arm and takes her to the operating theatre.

Abby tries protesting, but he doesn't listen to her. He keeps yelling at her to scrub up and get ready.

It has been a couple of years since she was in an operating room, but she gets scrubbed and dressed and meets Mr. Bronson in the theatre. He tells her the patient is an emergency appendectomy, and they have very little time to waste. She asks him for a moment to familiarize herself with the layout of the room and then she'll be ready.

After about an hour and a half, they are done. The patient is taken to recovery, and Mr. Bronson and Abby are washing up.

"You're a slow starter young lady, but once you get going you seem capable," he says without looking at her.

She thanks him for the complement and continues washing up. Mr. Bronson finishes and walks out without uttering another word to her. Abby finishes and walks out into the hallway.

As soon as she turns the corner, Matron is standing there.

"My office. Now!" is all Matron says. Abby puts her head down and slowly follows Matron to her office. Without asking if she wants one, Matron hands Abby a cup of tea. Abby is unsure of what to make of the situation, so she decides to stay quiet and let Matron do all the talking. Matron sits back in her chair and sips her tea. Abby can hear Matron's foot tapping on the floor as she sips her tea. Neither of them says a word. They just sit sipping their tea. Matron puts her empty cup on the desk, places the saucer on top of the cup, and leans further back in her chair. Abby is so nervous that her foot starts tapping. Matron's foot stops tapping, and now her finger starts to tap on the desk. She looks away from Abby and starts to speak.

She says, "I spoke with Mr. Bronson after the surgery. He told me you did a wonderful job. He said that whoever trained you was almost as good a surgeon as he is." Abby takes a sigh of relief and places her empty cup on the desk. Matron sits up straight, and her expression becomes very serious.

"You still don't work here; and yet, I find you wandering in and out of patients' rooms," Matron says.

Abby is about to say something, but Matron cuts her off. Matron pushes some papers in front of Abby, and says, "Sign this."

Abby asks her what the papers are, and Matron tells her it is her employment contract. Once she signs, she officially works in the hospital. Abby looks at the papers and notices her name "Abigail Alexis" on the top, and her address is listed as the nurses' home where Hyacinth lives. Abby takes a deep breath and summons up her courage. She reaches into her pocket and pulls out the picture of her mother. Without saying anything she hands the picture to Matron. Matron takes the picture, looks at it quickly. Then hands it back to Abby.

"I know my dear," Matron says. Abby is speechless. She slowly takes the picture and places it back in her pocket.

Matron stands up and slowly locks the door. She closes the curtains and turns to Abby.

"I know who you are Emilee, and you guessed who I am, but we must never ever tell a soul," Matron says as she opens her arms to hug Abby. Abby stands up and embraces her mother for the first time. With tears pouring down her cheeks, she can barely move. After a few moments they separate, and Abby simply says. "Why?"

Matron takes Abby's hand and says, "Not today, Child. As far as you are concerned I am Matron, and this conversation never happened. Now go home and come back ready for work tomorrow morning."

Abby's face drops as she tells Matron that she couldn't possibly be there in the morning. The earliest she could arrive would be one in the afternoon. Matron sits back at her desk and pulls out a book. She looks it over and tells Abby her hours will be from two in the afternoon until one in the morning. Abby smiles and goes on her way.

On her way back to the warehouse, Abby decides to stop at the nurses' home to see what her accommodations will be like. She feels she can rest there on the days she is too tired to walk back to the warehouse.

She knocks on the door and is greeted by the same women who greeted her the night she was brought there. She still couldn't remember her name, but remembered her as Sister. She tells Sister that she was just hired by the hospital, and Matron told her she would have a room here if she needed it. Sister tells her that all their rooms are occupied, but she will find her a bed in a room she can share with another nurse. Just as they start on their way upstairs, Hyacinth enters in through the front door. Abby and Sister turn to see who came in and as soon as Hyacinth and Abby's eyes lock, they run to each other and embrace in a big hug. Sister asks Hyacinth if she still has an empty bed in her room, and Hyacinth says she does. Sister turns to Abby and tells her it is all settled then. She would be sharing a room with Hyacinth. Sister backs away, and the two women race up the stairs to their room. Hyacinth tells Abby that she needs to change her clothes to get ready for her shift, but would love someone to talk to while she gets ready. Abby sits on her bed, and tells Hyacinth all about her day helping Mr. Bronson in the operating theater.

Hyacinth says that Abby is so lucky to be in surgery on her first day. She has been in the hospital for years, and hasn't been chosen for surgery yet. Hyacinth finishes getting dressed and bids Abby goodbye. As fast as she came in the front door is as fast as she goes back out, and Abby is alone in their room. She props herself up against the headboard and stares at the ceiling for a few minutes while she rehashes her day in the hospital over and over in her mind; talking to the patients, bumping into Matron, and going into the operating theatre.

She pauses her thoughts of the hospital and thinks about how Matron said she is her mother. Abby wants to run back to the hospital and talk to Matron about their conversation, but Matron made her promise not to tell anyone. She writes a note for Hyacinth asking her if there is anything that she needs, and places it on her pillow. She says goodbye to Sister walks slowly to the warehouse through the portal and is home.

When she gets back in her house, she pulls out her journal and writes down everything that happened to her today. After she finishes, she puts the journal away and reads a medical book. She still has dreams of becoming a doctor, and studies every moment that she is free.

Chapter 9 – Matron

June 13, 1979.

Emma Lee Alexis gave birth this day to a daughter. Eight pounds, seven ounces, and sixteen inches long. Emilee Abigail Alexis is her name. Emma Lee is fifteen years old, and not at all happy about having to take care of a new born child. She still thinks of herself as a child, and feels almost suicidal.

This is the beginning of a letter Matron is writing. She is alone in her office well past her time to go home. She often remains in her office after her shift ends. She lives alone and this hospital, and the people in it are her whole world. She pours a cup of tea and continues to write. Emma Lee met Daniel Alexis at a country and western concert in the small town where she lived. He was a rising star, and she lied to her parents so she could go to his show. Her parents thought she was at a sleepover with her friend Gloria. Gloria was with her at the concert.

After the show ended, Emma Lee and Gloria went around to the back door to see if they could get Mr. Alexis' autograph. Gloria had her camera and took a picture of Emma Lee with Daniel when they met him. Daniel was charming and Emma Lee was like putty in his hands. He asked her if she wanted to come to his hotel room for a pop, and she said yes. Gloria tried to talk her out of it, but Emma Lee went with Daniel to his room.

Matron takes a sip of tea, and says out loud. "You should have listened to Gloria, you fool."
She continues to write.

Emma Lee was only fourteen, and Daniel never bothered to ask her age. She slept with him that night. The next morning, they were awakened by someone banging on the door. When Daniel opened the door, three policemen and Emma Lee's father stormed into the room. Gloria had called her that morning and was afraid when her father said she hadn't come home yet. Her father said to Gloria that he thought Emma Lee was spending the night at her house. Gloria broke down in tears and told him about Emma Lee going to Daniel's hotel room. The police handcuffed Daniel and took him off to jail. Emma Lee was furious with her father, but even more upset with herself. Emma Lee's father told Daniel that he would spend the rest of his life in jail; if he wanted to be free, he would have to marry Emma Lee and get a decent job in town.

Daniel chose to marry Emma Lee, and they were married in the courthouse the next day. Daniel got a job working for Emma Lee's father in his furniture store. Daniel and Emma Lee lived in her father's house until the Lennon house was up for auction. They put in a low bid and were surprised that they won the house. It seems that there were rumors around town that the house was haunted and no one wanted to buy a haunted house. Not being from this town, Daniel never heard the rumors. They moved in and never once saw a ghost. Emma Lee kept attending school until she was eight months pregnant. When she dropped out of school, she was a straight A student and dreamed of going back to school to get her high school diploma. She thought she could continue on to college, but that would have to wait until the child was older.

One day, about a week after Emilee was born Gloria, came to visit. She mentioned to Emma Lee about getting a GED. Emma Lee asked her what that was, and Gloria explained to her that a GED was a high school diploma for people who never graduated from high school.

For the next couple of months, Emma Lee studied for her GED. She took the test and passed on her first attempt. Daniel wasn't happy about her getting more education. He wanted her to stay home and take care of Emilee.

The tension between them kept growing as the months went by. On Emilee's first birthday they held a party and invited some friends from church and some of Daniel's coworkers.

When the last of the party guests left, Daniel and Emma Lee had a major fight. He didn't like the way she was raising their daughter, and she didn't like the fact that he was rarely home. Emilee started to cry, and Emma Lee handed her to Daniel to figure out why. Daniel yelled at her because he didn't know what to do. Emma Lee walked out of the house and slammed the door. She stood in the garage and cried.

After crying for a few minutes. She decided she had enough. She found a piece of chalk on a table, and went to write a goodbye message on the wall. When she put the chalk to the wall, her hand went right through the wall. She didn't bother to pull it back, but just went on through the time portal. She didn't know it at the time, but when she went through the portal, she arrived in London England in 1910. She wandered the streets for what seemed like hours.

She wandered up to the nurses' home and there was a sign on the door advertising for new students. She went inside and was accepted into the class.

Four years later Emma Lee graduated first in her class and was offered a position in the hospital next to the nurses' home.

Emma Lee worked hard and worked her way up the ranks until she became the youngest Matron in the history of the hospital.

With a single tear rolling down her cheek, Matron looks over her letter then crumbles it and tosses it in the bin. She finishes her tea and leaves for home.

Abby is walking the halls of the hospital looking into a room occasionally. As she turns a corner, she finds herself outside Matron's office and the door is open. She goes inside to see if Matron is available to talk. The office is vacant, and there is still some tea in the pot. Abby pours herself a cup and sits in Matron's chair. Sipping her tea, she glances down and sees the letter crumpled in the waste bin. As she reaches for the letter, she hears footsteps outside the office. She puts the letter in her pocket and gulps down her tea. As she is putting the cup back, a maintenance man comes into the room and picks up the trash bin, but the bin is empty so he places it back where it was. Abby smiles at the man and says hello.

As soon as the man walks out of the office, Abby follows him and keeps walking until she is out of the hospital and goes back to the warehouse.

When she is home sitting at her kitchen table Abby pulls the letter out of her pocket and reads it.

With tears streaming down her cheeks, Abby places the letter in one of her father's photo albums. She looks out at the blank television screen and says, "Why, mom, why."

Chapter 10

July 7, 2012.

It is raining harder than Abby can remember in all her years living in Florida. She looks out the window and can barely see the road in front of her house. She stands there sipping her coffee and staring out at the pouring rain. Occasionally the lights from a passing vehicle can be seen slowly going past, but the rain is so thick she can't tell if it is a car or a truck. The lights in the house flicker a few times and then the power goes out.

"Glad I made the coffee before we lost power," Abby says out loud. She steps away from the window and sits on her father's chair to relax and sip her coffee.

Dozing off she thinks she hears the door in the garage slam shut. The sound startles her and she jumps to her feet. Thinking that perhaps someone is breaking in she grabs a knife from the kitchen and walks slowly to the garage door. As she is about to turn the doorknob there's a knock on the door. Startled, Abby shouts out. "I am armed, and have a black belt in karate.

A voice from the garage answers her. "When did you start studying karate."

"Who's there?" Abby shouts.

"It's Dave, may I come in? I'm soaked to the bone." Is the answer from the other side of the door.

Abby puts the knife down and opens the door. Dave is standing there looking like he just fell in a swimming pool. Abby smiles, laughs, and says, "You picked the perfect day to go for a stroll."

"I was trying to get to the church to check for any leaks when my car broke down. I walked all the way here from Jefferson Street," Dave says.

Without saying another word, Abby pours him a cup of coffee, grabs a towel, and her robe.

Dave goes into the bathroom to take off his wet clothes, and puts on the robe. It is a bit snug, but it covers most of him. He opens the bathroom door, and Abby is standing there with an empty laundry basket in her hands. She tells Dave to toss his wet things in the basket, so when the power comes back on, she can put them in the dryer.

Abby puts the basket in the laundry room and walks back to the kitchen. Dave is sitting at the table sipping his coffee.

Abby laughs and comments on how dapper he looks wearing her robe. Dave just smiles and continues to sip his coffee.

Abby and Dave move into the sitting room after they finish their coffee. Dave is very uncomfortable wearing Abby's robe and nothing else. He keeps fidgeting and adjusting the robe to cover himself. Abby suggests that she go through the portal and buy him some clothes. Dave likes the idea, and Abby finds a tape measure to take Dave's measurements.

After changing her clothes, Abby goes through the portal in search of menswear for Dave.

Dave sits in the sitting room switching his focus from the rain outside to Abby's photo albums. He really isn't paying much attention to either, but he is biding his time waiting for Abby's return.

Abby is wandering the streets of London looking for a men's store. After about twenty minutes of searching, she finally finds one. She asks the clerk for everything from underwear to a hat and coat. She picks out a nice conservative outfit so Dave could fit in wherever he roams around in the 1930s.

When Abby returns to her house, Dave is asleep on her father's chair. She places his new wardrobe on the bed in her father's room and starts to get ready for work.

While she is in the bathroom, Dave awakes and, thinking she isn't home yet, goes to go to the bathroom. He thinks it is odd that the door is closed, but opens it and is surprised to see Abby brushing her teeth. He shouts that he is sorry and slams the door shut.

Abby finishes brushing her teeth and goes to find Dave who is sitting in the sitting room. He keeps saying he is sorry and didn't realize that she had returned home. She tells him to forget about it and that his clothes are on her father's bed.

While Dave is getting dressed, the power comes back on.

Dave shouts out, "Thank you Lord."

Abby smiles and puts Dave's wet clothes in the dryer. Dave can hear the dryer, but he is too embarrassed to come out of her father's room. Abby calls out to him to come to the kitchen. He slowly walks into the kitchen looking like he just stepped out of a 1930s film.

Abby has him pose as she takes some photos of him. They both laugh as Abby prints out the pictures for him.

The rain has slowed, and Abby offers to drive Dave back to his car. Dave laughs and tells her he isn't about to go out dressed like he is. He asks if she minds if he waits for his clothes to dry and then he would go. She tells him it would take at least an hour for the dryer, so why not go for a stroll around the 1930s while he is waiting.

That sounds like a good idea to Dave and he says, "Why not."

Abby leads him into the garage and gives him some pound notes and a 1930s pocket watch. She explains to him that one hour in the past is equal to one minute in the present. So, he has plenty of time to wander around. They say goodbye as Dave goes through the portal and Abby goes about finishing getting herself ready for work. Just as she is about to turn the doorknob, her phone rings. She answers and is told that the road from her house to the hospital is washed out. She might as well stay home until she hears back from her supervisor. Abby hangs up the phone, smiles and says, "Why not."

She changes her clothes again and goes through the portal to look for Dave.

Not knowing where he might have wandered. Abby decides to stop in and see Douglas Lennon for a few minutes. Douglas is happy to see her, and they catch up on what is going on since they last saw each other. Abby asks him if he has seen a well-dressed stranger recently, and Douglas says he hasn't. They finish their chat, and Abby goes out looking for Dave.

As she leaves the pub, she sees Dave at the other end of the street. She calls to him and he spins around to see who called him. Upon seeing her he waves to her and walks towards her as she walks towards him. When they meet, Abby tells him about the road being closed, so she couldn't get to the hospital. She says that since she couldn't work today she might as well spend some time in the 1930s.

Abby offers to give Dave a guided tour, and he accepts. As they walk, Abby points out places of interest and things she likes to do and see. When they get to the toy store, Abby tells Dave all about her being the doll doctor and repairing broken dolls. She whispers softly that being a doll doctor is the next best thing to being a real doctor. After standing outside the toy store for a few minutes, they decide to go inside so Dave could look at some toys for his children. After spending more time than they should have in the toy store, Dave asks Abby if she is ready to go back to her house and check on his drying clothes.

They walk back slowly and take the scenic route through the park.

Upon exiting the park, they find themselves near the nurses' home. Abby asks Dave if he wouldn't mind waiting a few minutes while she goes inside to say hello to her friends. Dave sits on a bench and waits for Abby's return.

Dave is enjoying himself people watching when two hands are placed over his eyes, and a woman's voice says, "guess who?"

"I don't know. Maybe Abby?" Dave says.

"No. Guess again." She says with a slight giggle in her voice.

"Abby, this isn't funny." Dave says in a stern tone. The hands are removed, and a young, very well-dressed woman peers over Dave's shoulder. As soon as their eyes meet, the woman jumps back and apologizes over and over about the mistaken identity. She thought Dave was an old friend that she hadn't seen in months. Dave stands up and puts out his hand introducing himself as Dave Ivanovitch. She shakes his hand and introduces herself as Lady Ashley Taylor. He invites her to join him on the bench, so they may get to know each other better, but she declines. At that moment a Rolls Royce pulls up to them, and a chauffeur exits the car and opens the rear door. As Lady Ashley is entering the car, she pauses and turns to Dave.

"I am feeling a tad peckish. Would you care to join me for some lunch?" she asks him.

Dave thinks for a moment then tells her that he is waiting for his friend who is over at the nurses' home. If they can stop there so he can tell Abby where they are going, he would be glad to join her.

The car pulls up in front of the nurses' home just as Abby is exiting. Dave rolls down the window and calls her to attract her attention. Lady Ashley taps Dave on the shoulder and asks him if that is his friend. When Dave says she is, Lady Ashley begins to smile and calls Abby over to the car. Abby, looking confused at seeing Dave in the car, walks slowly to the car window. Lady Ashley asks Abby if she remembers her, and Abby thinks for a moment then says, "Emergency appendectomy."

"You do remember," Lady Ashley says with a big smile. "You must join us for lunch."

Abby, Dave and Lady Ashley have a light lunch and a few drinks too many. When they are finished, Dave offers to pay. Lady Ashley smiles says, "That's funny," and starts towards the door. Dave looks at Abby, confused. Abby shrugs her shoulders, and they follow Lady Ashley out the door. When they are in her car, Dave asks her how much they owe her for the lunch. Lady Ashley lets out a little laugh and says, "Nothing. My husband owns the establishment." They all smile as Lady Ashley asks them where she can take them. Abby asks her if she knows where The East End Pub is. Lady Ashley asks her chauffeur if he knows, and surprisingly he does.

When they arrive at the pub, Lady Ashley writes down her phone number and address for Abby and Dave. She tells them if they ever need anything to call her. She pauses and says that having lunch again would be nice when they are free. They say their goodbyes and walk slowly back through the portal.

As soon as they enter the house, they can hear the dryer still humming. The rain has let up to a trickle, and a hint of sunlight is starting to appear. Abby asks Dave to make some coffee while she changes her clothes in the garage.

She has her 1930s wardrobe in the garage near the portal, and she changes her clothes when she is about to go through and as soon as she comes back through the portal. She sits at the kitchen table as soon as she comes into the house.

"Where's my coffee?" she demands.

"I'm sorry your, Ladyship, but..." Before he can finish, she chimes in.

"No buts. I want coffee, and I want it now!" She demands. As he put the cups on the table, she laughs. "You just can't get good help these days."

"Nope," is all he says as he sits and sips his coffee.

Neither of them is in the mood to talk, so they sit in silence sipping their beverages. When the final drop is sipped, Dave jumps up and shouts, "Emily! She must be frantic not hearing from me."

Abby hands him her phone so he can call Emily and tell her he is safe and at her house. After a few minutes, he put his hand over the phone and says to Abby, "Well, I don't think she is jealous, but she isn't very happy either. She has heard about the road being closed, and doubts I'll be able to make it home. She wants to know if you could put me up for the night."

Abby tells him that it's not a problem; he can use her father's room. Dave tells Emily all is well, and he will call her tomorrow.

Abby hands Dave a new notebook and tells him to take notes of his travels into the past. She has been doing this for years, and the notebook really helps her keep her thoughts organized. Abby takes out her book, and the two of them spend the next hour and a half writing about their day. In the 1930s.

July 8, 2012.

Abby and Dave wake up early in order to take him to his car. When they arrive where he left it the day before, the car is gone. There is almost no one on the roads, so Abby drives Dave home. The drive between their houses usually takes about thirty-five minutes. With the roads closed, it takes them almost two hours. Dave thanks Abby for everything and says he will meet her at church. They say their goodbyes, and she drives off.

Emily is happy that Dave is home, but is upset that he never answered his phone. He takes his phone out of his pocket to show her that it is ruined from the rain. While he is getting ready for church, Emily tells him that Dominick called from the garage. He saw Dave's car on the side of the road and towed it to his shop. Dave is relieved to hear his car wasn't stolen.

Dave, Emily and their children sit in the back row of the chapel. Abby comes over and sits next to Emily and explains to her what happened the previous day. Hearing the same story from both of them puts Emily at ease. Abby thanks Emily for allowing Dave to help her at her house when she needs him. Emily tells her that she couldn't stop Dave from helping people if she tried. And that she won't try. No more is said about the previous day adventure, and they go their separate ways after church.

Abby is sitting on her father's chair eating a light lunch. She notices Dave's notebook and picks it up to read what he thought about their adventure. Of all the things he wrote, one thing stood out to her. He mentioned The East End Pub and thinking about going inside; but for some strange reason, feels he is not supposed to go in there, as if some form of energy is stopping him from entering the pub. Abby puts his book down and says out loud, "Perhaps it's a good thing not to go, Mr. Dave."

Abby gets herself ready to go back to 1932 to begin her shift at the hospital. Walking to the hospital is always one of her favorite things to do. Looking in the shop windows and smiling at the people she passes on the street, Abby can't help but wonder what life is like for all these people living during the "Great Depression." Passing a church, she sees the faces of the hungry people waiting to go inside for a bite to eat. She has never known what it's like to be hungry, so she really can't know how these people feel. Suddenly, a hand touches her on the shoulder. A cold chill travels down her spine as Abby turns to see who touched her, and is greeted by a smiling man's face. She doesn't recognize the man, but says "hello." The man says that she probably doesn't remember him, but they spoke a few weeks ago in the hospital. She came up to his bed, read his chart and smiled at him. They spent a few minutes chatting about his life and family. He tells her she is the only person in the hospital who took the time to get to know him and not just his ailment. Abby smiles and tells him that she is glad he is feeling better and jokingly says that she never wants to see him in the hospital again. He smiles and tells her to have a blessed day. She thanks him and wishes him the same.

About a block away from the hospital, she sees another line of hungry people waiting patiently for a handout at a storefront giving away bread and soup. Tears begin to swell up in her eyes as she feels empathy for all these hungry people. She has heard stories and seen pictures about these days, but seeing it face to face has touched a nerve. Abby stops and stares at the people and says out loud, "I will do something to help these people. I don't know what, but I will find a way to help them." Abby doesn't see Matron standing behind her as she said that.

"You are, my dear child. As a nurse in this hospital, you heal them so they can carry on one more day at a time," Matron says to Abby.

Abby turns and smiles at Matron.

"Good afternoon," Abby says.

Matron nods, and the two women walk into the hospital together.

It has been a quiet shift for Abby, and she is happy to be going home. She really enjoys her walks back and forth from the warehouse to the hospital. Quite often she wanders a different road to see new sights and experience new surroundings. She tries to carry a change purse full of farthings to hand out to people who ask her for something. The smiles on their faces is a great reward to her. Two small children approach her and ask her if she has anything to spare. Abby takes out her change purse to hand the children each a farthing when one of them tugs at her arm and some of the coins spill out onto the pavement. Abby says to them that if they help her to pick up the coins, she will give each of them three farthings. The children smile, and as fast as they can they pick up all the coins. Abby hands each of them four coins. They look down at their new-found wealth and tell Abby that she counted wrong. She promised three coins but gave them each four.

"I won't tell anyone if you don't," Abby says with a grin.

The children run off calling for their mother as Abby continues her walk. When she turns down a street she has been down dozens of times before, she notices a vacant building that for some reason never caught her eyes before. She peers in thru the windows and wonders why she never noticed this place before. There is a "for rent" sign in the window with a phone number on the bottom. She makes a mental note of the number and goes to The East End to ask Douglas if she can borrow his phone. Douglas hands her the phone and Abby dials the number. She explains that she wants to rent the space to open a soup kitchen. The man she is speaking to has a kind heart and offers her the space for one half of the amount he was asking.

After spending a couple of weeks with the help of Douglas, his daughter and friends the soup kitchen is ready. All she needs now is the food.

Abby calls Lady Ashley and asks her if she knows anyone who could help her with provisions. Lady Ashley says that her husband knows all the people Abby should deal with, and she would have him contact her at his earliest convenience.

Three weeks after signing the lease, her soup kitchen is ready to open. Abby decides to open on Tuesdays and Saturdays. Lady Ashley insists that she and her friends help

Abby on her first day. Abby also recruits some of the nurses to help her.

After a little over four hours, all the food has been served and the volunteers are happy and tired. Lady Ashley and her friends bid them goodbye and depart, leaving Abby and her nurse friends to clean up.

A little over a month later, the number of volunteers has dwindled to Abby, Hyacinth and an occasional one or two other nurses. Abby is frustrated and tired. Working two full time jobs and running the soup kitchen is wearing her out. She goes to the pub to ask Douglas for advice. He tells her to put a sign in the window looking for volunteers to help, and he will ask his daughter if she will help Abby. Abby takes Douglas' advice and puts a sign in the window.

When she arrives Tuesday morning to begin cooking, there is a que of about a dozen people outside the building. Abby recognizes most of the faces as people who regularly frequented the kitchen. Abby says hello as she walks past and opens the door. As soon as she is inside, the group of people follow her in and start to work. Abby falls to her knees and thanks the Lord. When she opens her eyes, she is face to face with the two children that she gave the farthings to. She smiles at them, and they ask her how they may help. Abby hugs them both and begins to cry.

By the time Abby regains her composure, everyone is busy making soup and baking bread. The children's mother comes over and thanks Abby for the money. Abby smiles and runs to the back of the kitchen to cry again.
She prays some more and blesses all the workers who showed up to help her. Hyacinth walks in and is floored by the people and activity. She sees Abby in the back and runs to her. Upon seeing Hyacinth Abby jumps to her feet and the two of them hug each other.

When the last bowl is washed Abby is exhausted and so happy she can't control herself. She grabs one of the children and starts to dance around the room. All the volunteers laugh at her and then join in dancing around the room.

Once she gets home, Abby is so tired that as soon as she sits on her father's chair she falls asleep.

Chapter 11

September 1, 2015

Emily got a phone call from her parents, and they made plans for her and the children to visit them for a couple of weeks. Because Dave has a few side jobs, he isn't able to go with them. Dave doesn't mind; and while Emily and the children are away visiting her parents, he calls Abby to see if she minds having him go with her to the 1930s.

Abby is happy for the company and tells Dave all about the soup kitchen. She tells him she could really use his help.

Dave has been struggling with headaches lately and has been taking painkillers. He keeps the bottle with him at all times, and takes a couple of pills every few hours to help ease the pain.

Abby and Dave return from a trip through the portal. Both of them are hungry and tired after spending the day working in the soup kitchen. Abby sits at the kitchen table and begins to write about their adventure. Dave is making coffee and calling for pizza delivery.

After they finish eating, Abby goes back to her writing. Dave gets out his notebook and begins to write about his day. After they finish writing and close their notebooks, Dave departs for his home.

Abby is off this evening and is happy just to sit and relax. While sitting on her father's chair, she sees Dave's notebook on the coffee table. She often wonders what he writes, and she opens his book to the present date and begins to read. Her eyes open wide as she reads what he wrote. "September 5, 2015. Abby and I went back to 1935 to feed the hungry at the soup kitchen she opened a couple of years ago. I enjoy spending time with her in the 1930s. She is a wonderful friend. We dished out soup and bread for a couple of hours until the soup and bread ran out. Abby apologized to the people who waited patiently for food but didn't receive any. Abby said she needed to do a half shift at the hospital and left me free to wander around town. While walking down an ally I had never seen before, I noticed the brickwork in one section of the wall looked different than the rest of the wall. I wondered if this was another time portal to a different place and time. I went to touch the wall, and my hand passed right through it. It was a portal. I took a deep breath and walked through. On the other side, I found myself in a place so foreign-looking yet somehow familiar. I felt as though I was in one of those movies about ancient Rome. I couldn't understand a single word anyone was saying. As people noticed me, they stopped and stared. Some were touching me and bowing down. I heard the crack of a whip and someone shouting. All the people started to clear the middle of the road as if for a parade. There was shouting and fists being held high. I joined the crowd and shouted and held up my fist. In the distance, I could see what looked like Roman soldiers cracking whips and shouting at the people along the street. As they approached closer to me, I could see a man covered with fresh sores and blood. He was dragging a large wood object and kept falling to his knees. He fell and could not lift himself. One of the guards grabbed a bystander by the arm and forced him to carry the large wooden object. Suddenly, I had a horrible and excited feeling that I was watching the crucifixion of Jesus Christ.

I slapped my face to see if I was dreaming. Not dreaming. Wide awake. I screamed "Yeshua ha Mashiach" as he walked passed me. He turned and looked at me; and as our eyes met, with a slight smile he nodded towards me.

I couldn't get close to see him nailed to the cross because of the large crowd; but as the crowd slowly dispersed, I walked up to him. I didn't know at that moment whether to be happy or sad. Happy in the knowledge that in three days he will rise again, but sad that he is enduring so much pain for me and my sins. I watched people spit at him and shout at him and call him names. Others prayed and cried for him. I took my phone out to take his picture. His eyes caught mine and he slowly blinked and shook his head from left to right as if to say don't do it. I put my phone away and walked closer to him. The headache returned and I could hardly focus my eyes. I took the bottle of pills from my pocket, and poured the last two pills onto my hand. Someone jostled my arm and the pills fell to the ground getting trampled into the dirt. All at once I thought of the woman who had the issue of blood and touched him to be healed. I reached out to touch him and one of the Roman guards hit my hand. I noticed the blood dripping from him onto the ground, and held out the empty pill container to catch some of the Lord's blood. After catching a few drops of his blood, I was again hit by a Roman guard. I stepped back prayed and touched the blood in the container. At that instant, my headache was gone. I fell to my knees, prayed again and walked slowly back to the portal to 1935.

I doubt I will ever tell Abby about this. She would never believe me anyway.

Abby closes the notebook and sits back in the chair staring up at the ceiling and thinking if this is a real story or something Dave just made up. After thinking for a few minutes, she goes into her garage to look at Dave's trousers. If he indeed knelt on the dirt there would be traces of dirt on his trousers. As she pulls the trousers from their hanger, the painkiller bottle falls out of the pocket onto the floor. Her hands are shaking as she bends down to pick it up. Her hands are shaking so much she could barely hold the bottle. She holds it tightly in her hand and walks back into the house. She sits at the kitchen table and puts the bottle down in the middle of the table.

As Abby is reaching for the bottle to open it, her telephone rings startling her. She knocks the bottle on its side as she gets up to answer the phone. It's her supervisor; she wants to know if Abby can cover another nurse's shift tonight. Abby says she will and hangs up the phone. She turns to the table to get the bottle, and it is no longer on the table. She searches the chairs and the floor, but the bottle has vanished. She spends the next fifteen minutes looking for the bottle but cannot find it anywhere. She finally gives up the search and gets ready to go to work.

While Abby is at work, Dave stops by the house to look for the bottle in his trousers. He reaches into the pocket that the bottle was in and discovers a giant hole in the pocket. Disappointed at the loss of the bottle, Dave goes back home.

Chapter 12

December 30, 2018.

Emily and Dave are planning a last-minute New Years Eve party, and Dave asks Emily if it is okay for him to invite Abby. Emily smiles and says, "the more the merrier." After the invite calls are made. they have thirty people who said they would attend.

Emily makes up a shopping list for Dave to go out and purchase all the food and supplies they need.

Dave's last stop is Abby's house. Her car is in the drive, but that doesn't mean she will be home. He goes into the garage and knocks on the door to the house. Abby comes to the door wearing her pajamas and robe. Her eyes are red, and it appears to Dave that she has been crying. He says he can't stay long and asks her if she would like to come to a party tomorrow night.

She doesn't say anything, but turns and walks back to the kitchen table. She sits down and sips her coffee that has become cold from sitting on the table too long. Dave asks her what is wrong, but she doesn't answer him. She just takes another sip of coffee and stares into space. Dave stands behind her and puts his hands on her shoulders. He says a prayer for her and sits down across from her at the table. For a few minutes nothing is said. Abby occasionally takes a sip of coffee and is still staring into space.

When her cup is empty, she looks Dave in the eyes and begins to cry. He stretches out his hands on the table, and Abby takes hold of his hands. After a few more minutes, she begins to speak.

"I had a rough day in the hospital in the 1930s. A woman who has been helping me in the soup kitchen was brought in by ambulance. We could tell instantly that she had been severely beaten. We ran some tests and comforted her as best we could. When I was alone with her, I asked her what happened. She turned away from me and covered her face with her hands. I walked around the bed and slowly uncovered her face. I didn't say anything. I just smiled and waited for her to speak. After a few minutes, she began to tell me that it was all her fault. She never should have said anything. I asked her what happened. She said her husband came home early from work. She asked him why he was so early. He screamed at her to mind her own business and give him some money. She told him the only money they had needed to buy food for the children. That was the first time he hit her. She cried and begged him not to hit her again. He grabbed her by the arm and told her he would break it off if she didn't give him the money. She reached into her apron pocket and pulled out the pence that she had saved. He hit her across the face and grabbed the money from her hand. Again, she begged him that they needed the money for food. He hit her again and left her flat on the floor as he slammed the door shut.

A few hours later, he came home drunk and demanded his supper. She told him she was sorry that they only had soup and no bread. He started yelling and shouting then threw the soup bowls across the room and started to pummel her like a fighter in the ring. When he was finished he left her for dead and disappeared. A neighbor coming home from work seeing their door open looked inside and saw her on the floor. The neighbor called for the ambulance, and she stopped talking. Her eyes rolled back and she passed away from her injuries."

Dave gets up, brings her a box of tissues then sits back down.

Abby continues. "There was nothing I could do! All I could do was sit there and watch her die. I prayed for her. I tried CPR. There was nothing I could do for her. I failed her. I failed her. I am a failure."

Dave takes her hands again and prays for her.

They sit silently for a few minutes. Abby regains her composure and asks him why he is visiting her. Not that she minds, and she really needs the company. Dave tells her about the party; and before she could say anything, he tells her that she needs to come. It will be good for her. He slowly rises and gives her a little smile.

"You aren't a failure. Her husband is, um or was, (whatever) a failure." Dave says as he walks out the door. Abby sits there staring at the box of tissues for about ten minutes. Then she jumps up, picks up a medical book and begins to study. "This will never happen to me again," she says as she reads all about physical abuse and blunt force trauma.

December 31, 2018.

The alarm on the microwave is chiming and the kitchen of Emily and Dave is abuzz with activity. Emily looks at the time and exclaims. "It's 7:15 they will be arriving soon, and we are no-where near ready."

Dave tells her not to worry; everything will be fine. The doorbell rings, and Emily goes to see who it is. Abby is the first to arrive, and she brought with her a large tray of cookies and a bottle of champagne. Emily gives her a big hug, and the cookies almost fall. The two women catch the tray and laugh a little. Emily can see Abby's eyes are still red from crying, but doesn't say anything to her. She mentions it to Dave, and he tells her that he knows and they already prayed about it.

January 1, 2019.

The last of the revelers are heading out the door as Emily is waving goodbye. Dave is in the kitchen cleaning up. Emily comes over to Dave and gives him a hug and a kiss. Happy Near Year," she says with a smile.

"That was fun, tiring but fun." Dave says to her.

"Let's just go to bed. We can finish with this tomorrow." Emily says.

Dave agrees, and the two of them head out of the kitchen into the sitting room. They notice that Abby hasn't left and is asleep on the sofa. Emily puts her finger to her lips for them to be quiet. She goes into the linen closet and retrieves a blanket and pillow for Abby.

Emily is the first to awake in the morning, and she goes to see how Abby is doing. Abby is no longer asleep on the sofa, and there is the sound of running water coming from the kitchen. Emily thinks Dave is finishing the cleanup from last night, and she calls out to him. "I didn't know you were up honey." She calls out towards the kitchen.

"I just got up, darling." the answer from the kitchen in a woman's voice. As Emily enters the kitchen Abby is just finishing the cleanup. She looks at Emily and the two of them let out a laugh. Dave staggers into the kitchen seeing Emily and Abby laughing.

"You're feeling better today, I see." Dave says to Abby.

"Much better." Abby replies.

"Did you make coffee?" Dave asks as Emily hits him in the arm.

"As a matter-of-fact, I did." Abby says pointing to the coffee pot.

Emily and Dave are in a mock battle, elbowing each other to get to the coffee first. Abby starts to tickle Dave, and Emily reaches the pot first. She lifts the pot up high and proclaims herself the winner. The three of them laugh as they prepare their cups.

Sitting at the table sipping their coffee, Abby is the first one to start to speak, "Thank you for letting me sleep on your sofa last night." She says as she takes a sip and continues, "I guess I needed a good night's sleep after the day I had."

Dave motions to Emily not to ask about her day, and she catches on. Emily asks her what her plans for the day are, and Abby says that she has none.

"Just rest," she says.

Emily says to Abby that she needs to go shopping and would love some non-Dave company. The women smile and giggle as Dave turns his chair to face away from the two of them.

Abby and Emily head out to the mall, leaving Dave alone. He checks on their teenagers, and they have already gone out. Dave picks up the newspaper and starts reading a story about a WWII veteran from their town. He finishes the article and puts the paper down on the table. Dave is thinking about what he wants to do with the rest of his day, and decides to go through the portal and wander around in 1939.

It's late afternoon when Dave arrives in London. It's cool but not cold, and Dave is not used to the cold being from Florida. He is wearing the hat and coat that Abby purchased for him, but is still cold. He wanders into a men's haberdashery and inquires about a warmer coat and some gloves. He purchases the warmest coat they have and a nice pair of leather gloves. He thinks that twenty pounds is a bit extravagant but by today's standards it's not a bad price to pay. Happy with his warmer coat and gloves he smiles as he walks down the street. As he turns the corner, a large Rolls Royce pulls up beside him. The window rolls down and Lady Ashley appears in the window.

"Can we offer you a lift, my friend?" Lady Ashley asks.

Dave is a little startled, but asks her where she is heading as he has no plans and is open to any suggestions.

"Ooh! A man after my own heart." She exclaims. Then she pauses and askes Dave if he is in the mood for a few cocktails? Without thinking, Dave climbs into the car with Lady Ashley and says, "Why not." As the car starts to move, Dave realizes that he hasn't had breakfast yet. Only a couple of cups of coffee. Although it is afternoon in London, back home it is still morning.

"Could we have a little bite to eat first?" Dave asks. Lady Ashley agrees, and they stop at her husband's place. The moment they are seated, a waiter approaches them and asks for their order. Lady Ashley, without consulting Dave, orders for both of them.

"I hope you don't mind that I ordered for you. I simply love the halibut here," she says as she waves to someone across the room. The man she is waving to approaches the table, and Lady Ashley introduces him to

Dave as Roger, her husband. Dave stands and shakes hands with Roger and invites him to join them. Roger cordially declines, but tells Dave that he has heard all about Dave and Abby and what lovely friends they are for his wife. As he is walking away, Roger kisses Lady Ashley's hand and says, "Enjoy your halibut." She blows him a kiss, and he disappears into the back of the room. As soon as Roger is out of sight, the waiter is at their table with a tray of cocktails. Lady Ashley picks up a glass and says, "To good friends." Dave lifts a glass, and they clink their glasses and sip their cocktails.

"That was delicious." Dave says, as he puts his knife and fork on his plate. Lady Ashley simply smiles and orders them another round of cocktails.

When they finish their cocktails, Roger appears back at their table. He hands Dave a card and asks how Dave enjoyed the meal.

"Delicious," Dave says as he reaches for the card. One side of the card has the name and address of the restaurant, and the other side has printed on it, "V.I.P." Roger says to Dave that anytime he is in the neighborhood to stop in, and whatever he wants is on the house. Dave is about to say that he cannot accept the offer, but Roger has already disappeared. Lady Ashley and Dave walk out together arm in arm because they both had too much to drink and are a little unsteady on their feet. They climb into her car, and she asks Dave where they can drop him off.

"The East End Pub, if you don't mind," Dave says. They say their goodbyes and see you soon, and the car speeds off and out of sight. Dave goes back through the portal and sits in Abby's garage.

Still a little drunk, he closes his eyes and falls asleep on a chair in the garage.

Abby arrives in her garage and sees Dave asleep on her chair. She smiles and contemplates whether to wake him or let him sleep. She decides to wake him by nudging him gently. That isn't working, so she turns on the radio and keeps raising the volume until he starts to wake up. He opens his eyes and is startled by Abby's presence in front of him. He jumps to his feet and trips and falls, causing both of them to break out laughing. Dave regains his composure and climbs up to his feet. Abby invites him inside for some coffee, and he agrees. They sit and stare at each other listening to the coffee maker spurtle and drip their favorite liquid into the carafe. Abby pours them each a cup and sits back down. She asks Dave how his trip to 1939 was, and he tells her all about the new coat and meeting Lady Ashley and

Roger. Abby corrects him telling him that it's Lord Roger and not just Roger. Dave stands, bows and apologizes, calling Abby "her Ladyship." Abby laughs and holds out her hand for him to kiss her ring. He goes down on one knee and gently takes her hand and kisses her ring, pledging his undying loyalty to her kingdom. Abby picks up her coffee cup and places it on each of his shoulders, knighting him Sir Dave of the portal. They both laugh as Dave sits back down, and they finish their coffee. Abby reminds Dave to write his adventure in his notebook before he leaves, and he does.

After Dave leaves, Abby picks up her medical book and turns to the bookmarked page. Her bookmark is the business card she received from Dr. Bryon Jones some years ago. She looks at the card and decides to go look him up and see if he would help her attend medical school.

Chapter 13

Matron is sitting at her desk, sipping a cup of tea as Abby knocks on the office door.

"Come in," Matron says with a slight smile. Abby asks her if she remembers Dr. Bryon Jones, and Matron says that she speaks with him frequently. Abby asks Matron if she could ask him to pull some strings and get her admitted into the medical school. Matron doesn't say anything but goes to the teapot and pours Abby a cup. Abby thanks her for the tea, and Matron sits back down. There is silence as the two women sit and sip their tea. Matron has mentioned to Abby in the past that she doesn't like to converse while she sips her tea. It's her quiet time away from the pressures of the hospital. When her cup is empty, Matron places the saucer on top of the cup. This is her signal that she is ready to talk. Matron is not in the habit of smiling, but occasionally she will smile at Abby. Abby finishes her tea and places the cup on the desk. Matron opens her desk drawer and pulls out a piece of paper and hands it to Abby. As she hands the paper to Abby, Matron tells her that Dr. Jones has been waiting for her to contact him. He thinks she would make a wonderful doctor. Abby is at a loss for words, as she looks over the paper that Matron just handed her. The paper is a document from Dr. Jones recommending Abby for admission to the medical school.

"All you had to do was ask," Matron tells her. "Now go on your way; I must get back to work."

Abby thanks Matron and is beaming as she skips out of the hospital on her way to the medical school.

The medical school is about a one mile walk from the hospital, and it takes Abby almost no time at all to get there. She is so excited she can barely control her enthusiasm. When she walks in the building she is greeted by a man at a desk. She asks to see Dr. Jones, and the man asks her to wait on a bench against the wall. After about fifteen minutes, Dr. Jones appears from down the hall. He recognizes Abby as soon as he sees her, and (ignoring the man at the desk) goes straight to Abby and pulls her from the bench and gives her a hug. Abby doesn't know what to do, but lets him hug her.

"That was for saving me from that awful doctor. We had him transferred to India. Hopefully, he straightens out while he is there." Dr. Jones says.

He leads Abby to his office and asks her to sit. As she is about to sit down, she hands him the paper that Matron gave her. He glances quickly at the paper and says, "about time you got here. I've been waiting for you ever since we first met."

Abby lets out a little giggle and a grin then composes herself quickly. She is unsure of the decorum and rules she must follow.

Doctor Jones explains all the tests and applications she must take and fill out before she can enter the school officially. But with his recommendation, she will be able to attend classes while the admitting process is being completed. Abby tells him she doesn't know how to thank him, and Dr. Jones tells her the only way for her to thank him is to become the best doctor she can. Abby smiles, stands and tells him she will be the best doctor in her class.

They both smile, shake hands, and Abby is escorted outside carrying a stack of forms that need to be filled out as soon as possible.

Abby is sitting at her kitchen table which is covered with the forms that Dr. Jones gave her to fill out. She is having a difficult time filling in the forms with the simple questions; Date of birth, address, telephone number, school records and college transcripts. She laughs out loud thinking that if she tells them the truth she will be escorted to the insane asylum. She pauses her work, and goes to look for her school records. She goes into the garage because all her files are in a cabinet in the garage. She pulls out file folder after file folder until she finds the one she is looking for. The folders she didn't need at the moment are left strewn all over the floor. She tosses the folder on top of the forms on the table and gets herself ready to go to work.

January 5, 2019.

Abby still has her table covered with papers and has no idea how to fill out the medical school entrance forms. While she gets the coffee maker ready, there is a knock on the door to the garage.

"Who is it?" Abby calls out.

"Dave." The voice from the other side of the door responds. Happy to have someone to bounce ideas off of, Abby lets Dave in and directs him to the table.

"I see filing is not your strong suit," Dave says with a slight grin.

"I need to fill out these forms to enter medical school in 1939," Abby says to him. She pauses then continues. "I don't know how to answer these questions," she says as she hands Dave the forms.

Dave stares at the forms for a couple of minutes then says. "Do you have any friends in 1939 that are not related to the hospital?"

Abby thinks for a moment, then smiles and shouts out, "Douglas!"

Dave looks quizzingly at her and asks her who Douglas is. She thinks for a moment and then tells him that he is a friend in 1939. Dave tells her that she has never mentioned him before, and Abby just smiles and says that he is just a friend and there is no need to get jealous. Dave looks at her, tilting his head and squinting his eyes.

"Jealous," he says. "I don't think so. I'm happily married to Emily in case you forgot." There is a moment of silence then they both laugh. Abby gathers up her papers and heads out to the garage. Dave sees the recently brewed coffee and pours himself a cup.

"Might as well," he says.

"What?" A shout comes from the garage.

"Stealing a cup of coffee. Call the police." Dave shouts back. He waits for an answer, but there isn't one. He slowly walks to the garage and notices Abby is already gone. He drinks half his cup and tries to remember why he came to Abby's house in the first place. He leaves her a note to call him, and he leaves for home.

Chapter 14

January 5, 2019

Abby walks into the East End to see Douglas. The pub is busy, and Douglas is behind the bar with his daughter Emilie serving customers. Abby is unsure whether to interrupt them or not. Douglas sees her, smiles and calls her over to him. As he is about to introduce Emilie to Abby, Emilie walks away to the other side of the pub to serve a customer. Douglas looks at Abby and says, "Next time I suppose." Abby shrugs her shoulders and goes right into the reason for her visit. She asks Douglas if she can use his pub address as her address for her medical school application. Douglas smiles and asks to see the papers. He takes out a pen and fills in the address and telephone number for her. As he is writing, he sees the date of birth section. He fills it in with Emilie's date and place of birth. He smiles and says, "that they appear the same age so no one will know the difference." When he gets to the school records section, he puts his pen down and says to Abby that he has no answers for that. Abby thanks Douglas for his help, smiles and tells him that she knows someone who can help her with that.

Douglas offers her a drink, but before he has a chance to grab a glass, Abby is gone.

Abby knocks on the door of Matron's office, but receives no answer. As she stands there contemplating her next move, a maintenance man approaches her. She asks him if he has seen Matron recently, and the man responds that he saw her about fifteen minutes ago in the emergency room. Abby thanks the man and heads off to the emergency room.

Abby looks around and does not see Matron anywhere, so she walks up to the nurse at the desk, and asks her if she has seen Matron recently. The nurse tells her that Matron just went outside. She says that if Abby hurries she may be able to catch her up.

Abby races out the door into the driveway. She sees Matron in the distance speaking with one of the doctors Abby has not worked with yet. It looks like a very serious conversation, and as Abby is walking towards them Matron sees her, and lifts her hand, making a stop motion. Their conversation must be extremely private to be holding it in the parking lot. Abby leans against the building and waits for them to end their conversation.

After about ten minutes, Matron motions for Abby to approach them. When she is close enough to speak, the doctor reaches out his hand and introduces himself to Abby as Dr. Richards, the new head of the hospital. Abby shakes his hand and introduces herself to him. He smiles, tells her it is nice to meet her, and he is looking forward to working with her. He thanks Matron for her time and he walks towards the hospital entrance. Matron turns to Abby and asks her what is so important that she had to track her down in the car park. Abby shows Matron the application to medical school, and Matron smiles a slight smile.

"In my office, not out here," is all Matron says.

After they enter Matron's office, Abby asks if Matron would like a cup of tea. She simply shakes her head yes and sits down. Abby pours them each a cup and sits opposite Matron. Abby places her application on the desk and slowly sips her tea waiting for the signal that Matron is ready to talk.

Matron places the saucer on top of her cup and picks up the application. She is holding it in front of her face, and Abby cannot see Matron's face. Abby sits up and asks if Matron sees the problem she is having.

"Schooling," Matron says.

She places the application on her desk and fills in the school information for Abby. She finishes writing and hands the application back to Abby.

Matron sits back in her chair giving the slightest hint of a grin and says, "I am so proud of you, my child. Now go and learn how to be the best doctor England has ever known." She pauses and continues, "just don't neglect your work here while you are studying."

Abby stands and puts her arms out to give Matron a hug. Matron just sits back in her chair and shakes her head. Abby thanks Matron for her help and slowly leaves her office.

After dropping the application off at the medical school, Abby stops at the East End to grab a drink and settle her nerves. It's been a hectic few hours, and she feels the need for some liquid nerve settling. Douglas is happy to see her again and ignores the rest of his customers to give Abby his full attention.

Abby finishes her drink and her conversation with Douglas. She says goodbye and goes back through the portal to her home.

Chapter 15

Thursday February 2, 2019.

Abby wakes up after a very restful sleep. She lies on her bed and contemplates what she wants to do before she has to go to school and then to work. Working two full-time jobs and attending medical school is starting to wear her down. She has been drinking more than she wants to, but needs something to calm her nerves. In 1939, she only has the occasional beer at the East End; but in 2019, she has some stronger drinks in her home. She looks at her clock and calculates the time difference.

"Time to get started," she says to her dolls. She has them lined up on the window sill and talks to them from time to time. As she is about to brush her teeth, the phone rings. She answers with a cheerful hello and is silent for the rest of the call. She says, "Thank you" and then "Goodbye" and hangs up the phone. She rushes to her dolls and tells them her request to switch from full-time to part-time has been approved. A weight has been lifted from her as now she only has to work three days a week in 2019. That gives her more time to study for medical school. It is still difficult working six eight hour shifts at the hospital in 1939 and then rushing to school, but she loves it, and that makes her happy.

When Matron saw that Abby was accepted to medical school, she changed Abby's hours from 2:00 pm to 2:00 am. Abby now works from 8:00 pm to 4:00 am. When her shift ends, she goes to the nurses' housing, changes her clothes, grabs a quick breakfast, studies a little and runs to the medical school. If she was living in 1939, she would only have about four hours of sleep a night, but since she goes back to 2019 after school, she has only spent about twenty minutes in 1939. This gives her all the time she needs to sleep and work at the hospital in 2019.

Abby is finishing getting ready to go to 1939, and she pauses to look outside. It is a warm sunny day, and she steps outside to enjoy a few minutes of the Florida sunshine. She looks at her watch and realizes that she has to leave. She grabs her purse; and without thinking, goes through the portal. When she enters the warehouse, it is bitter cold, and Abby neglected to wear her coat and hat. She stepped out of the warehouse into two inches of fresh snow. The snow is still falling, and Abby is freezing. She pauses for a moment to figure if she has time to go back and get her hat and coat. Being late, she runs as fast as she can to the hospital, slipping and falling a number of times on her way. Abby enters the hospital freezing, teeth chattering and covered with snow. She races to the kitchen for a cup of tea to warm herself and bumps into Matron. Matron looks her over and says, "I didn't know we were hiring snow monsters."

Abby giggles and says, "You are the last to know."

Matron joins her for a cup of tea and fills her in on the hospital happenings of the day. They say goodbye, and Abby heads off to work.

It is an easy night, and Abby is glad it's over. She rushes to the nurses' home to change and bumps into Hyacinth. They have a nice chat about the hospital, but Abby cuts the conversation short.

"I have to get to school," she says as she races down the stairs to the dining hall. She eats her porridge and is off to school.

Entering the medical school, Abby always smiles. This has been her lifelong dream, and she is doing it. After entering the building, she checks the board for her test results. A voice behind her tells her she aced another one. Abby smiles and turns quickly. She walks directly into Dr. Jones, almost knocking him down.

"Slow down young lady," he says with a grin. "I need to see you in my office after your class." Abby doesn't answer him, but is concerned. He has never wanted to see her before. She thinks the worst and is no longer smiling. She has a hard time concentrating on the lecture, and is the first one out the door when it is through. She is torn between racing to Dr. Jones office and taking her time. As she is walking, her anatomy and physiology professor sees her in the hall. He calls he name, and Abby stops in her tracks.

"What now," she thinks.

"I just want to tell you that you are perhaps the brightest student I have ever had in my class, and it is a pleasure to have you." He says.

Abby thanks him and continues to Dr. Jones' office. She is directed to sit down and wait for Dr. Jones to return. She is told he will be right back. She is constantly fidgeting in her chair and can't sit still. She sits and stands and sits and stands over and over. She drops her purse and spills the contents just as Dr. Jones enters the office.

"Relax, Miss Alexis," he says to her as he takes his seat. He patiently waits for her to pick up her spilled items and take her seat. She takes a deep breath and prepares herself for the worst.

Before he begins to speak, his secretary brings them each a cup of tea. "A good sign," Abby thinks.

"I wanted to speak with you, Miss Alexis because every single one of your professors has told me the same thing about you. You are number one in your class. As a matter of fact, no other student in the history of this school has ever scored such high marks on all their exams. Because of this, we are creating an accelerated program for you. Each of your professors is creating a special set of programs and exams for you to take. The passing grade for each exam will be in the high nineties. If you feel up to the challenge, we will begin on Monday." He pauses and takes a sip of his tea.

"I don't know what to say," Abby replies.

"A simple I am ready, I suppose, would suffice." He answers.

Abby thanks Dr. Jones, and heads out of the school.

February 6, 1939. Monday morning.

It was a slow night in the hospital, so Abby was able to read some of her medical books to prepare herself for what was to come when she arrives at school. She races out of the hospital and changes her clothes at the nurses' housing. A quick bite to eat, and she is off to school. Dr. Jones is at the front desk to greet her, and he leads her to a small private room. He asks her to wait for a few minutes as her professor is running a little late. As soon as Dr. Jones exits the room, the professor enters with a small stack of papers. He places the papers on her desk and proceeds to explain what they are going to do today. This test is merely to determine her level of knowledge on the subject matter. He tells her she has four hours to complete the exam, and then he will return with further instructions. He looks at his watch points at her and says, "Begin."

Abby turns over the papers and reads the heading. "Immunology, Hematology, Inflammation and Infectious Disease." Abby smiles as she recalls the subject matter from when she was in nursing school.

She takes her time answering all the questions to make sure she doesn't make any mistakes; and after two and a half hours, she places the papers face down on her desk and sits back smiling. A few moments later the professor peeks into the room and sees that Abby is finished. He asks her if she is done, or just taking a breather. She tells him she is done and could use a break to visit the ladies. He takes the papers from her desk and takes them to his office to grade them.

When Abby returns from the ladies, the professor is gone, and the room is empty. Not knowing where he went or what to do, Abby sits at her desk and waits. After about fifteen minutes, Dr. Jones appears at the doorway. He asks her if she completed the exam and she says that she did, but wasn't informed of what to do next. Dr. Jones tells her to go on with her normal class schedule, and he walks with her to her next class. As they part company he asks, her to stop at his office on her way out after her last class.

Moments after her last class, Abby is waiting outside Dr. Jones' office. There are three other people ahead of her, and she is nervous as she waits to see him. Twenty minutes pass, and Abby is still waiting to see Dr. Jones. When it's her turn to go into his office, the professor who administered her test rushes in front of her and closes the door in her face. Abby can hear the two men's voices through the door, but cannot make out what they are talking about. Suddenly the door flies open, and the professor rushes past Abby almost knocking into her. She pauses for a moment to catch her breath when Dr. Jones calls to her. She slowly walks into the office and closes the door behind her. Dr. Jones motions for her to sit down as he is reading some papers. He puts the papers down and looks almost staring into Abby's eyes.

"How do you do it?" he asks her.

"Do what?" she answers.

"Not only finish a four-hour test in two and a half hours, but score a perfect one hundred percent. Professor Charles insists that you cheated." He walks around his desk and sits on the edge inches from Abby. "Did you cheat?"

"No sir," she shouts out, standing and walking to the other end of the office to give herself some space.

"We don't get many females in our school, and Mr. Charles is against females becoming doctors. Be on your best behavior around him. No go out and celebrate how well you did on your exam. Tomorrows will be harder I'm sure."

Abby thanks Dr. Jones and heads back to the warehouse as fast as she can. Once inside her house, she plops on her father's chair with a glass of wine to relax.

The maternity ward is busier than usual this evening, and Abby has no time to stop and study. Everyone is blaming the full moon for the over-capacity number of babies being born this evening. They even have a hospital record of three sets of triplets. When her shift ends, Abby is so exhausted she can barely move. She pulls her car into her driveway and turns off the engine. She sits staring at the house in front of her to tired to move. After about ten minutes, she finally forces herself to go inside the house. She has no time to waste as she has to prepare for school. She sets up the coffee maker and takes a cool shower. She pours a cup of coffee before she even gets dressed. She smiles and thinks now would not be a good time for Dave to show up unannounced. There is a knock on the door, and she spills her coffee, running to get her bathrobe and answer the door. She is thinking it must be Dave and he forgot his key. She opens the door to find two Jehovah's Witnesses. She puts her hand on her face says, "Not today." And slams the door shut. She cleans up the coffee spill, and the phone rings. She looks at the phone and ignores it. After getting dressed she plays the phone message just in case it's important.

"Hello Abby, this is Emily. Dave wanted me to call you to ask if would like to join us for a Valentines masquerade party. Call me when you get this message, and let me know." Abby looks at the machine for a moment and then races to the garage and through the portal. As she exits the warehouse, the cold February air hits her face and revives her. She walks briskly to the medical school for her second exam. Like the previous day, Dr. Jones is there to greet her as she enters, and he shows her to the room for her second exam. As she is removing her coat, Professor Gotlieb enters the room. He stands in the doorway waiting for her to take her seat. Once she is seated, he places a stack of paper on her desk. He doesn't make eye contact with her, but looks at his watch.

"You have five hours to complete this exam, and I will be checking in on you to be sure you are not cheating like yesterday." He says in a stern monotone voice.

Abby thinks about arguing with him about the fact that she didn't cheat, but feels that would be a useless waste of energy.

"You may begin," he says.

Abby turns the papers over and reads the heading. "OB/GYN." Is all that is typed across the top of the page. Abby smiles and begins answering the questions. Abby is not as slow answering the questions as yesterday. This is one of her favorite fields, and she knows it. Professor Gotlieb is standing in the doorway watching her.

Two and a half hours later, and Abby turns the papers over. "Done." She says to the professor who watched her the entire time. He quickly snatches the papers from her desk and heads off down the hallway. Abby spends the rest of her day walking on air. She aced the test, and she knows it.

After her last class, she goes to Dr. Jones' office to hear the results. Unlike the previous day there is no one else there to see Dr. Jones. She knocks on the door and is called into the office. Dr. Jones, Professor Gotlieb and Mr. Charles are standing in a row.

"Please sit," Dr. Jones requests of her.

Abby pushes the chair back a couple of feet and sits down.

"I watched you the entire time you were taking my test, and I can attest that you could not have cheated." You, my dear are going to make a wonderful doctor." Professor Gotlieb says and walks out of the office. Dr. Jones nudges Mr. Charles, and Mr. Charles extends his hand. Abby shakes his hand as he says, "I am sorry I accused you of cheating. You have proven that you are not just another female trying to make a statement. You really do want to be a doctor." After saying this he also exits the office. Dr. Jones smiles at Abby and also shakes her hand.

"Keep up the good work. Your next exam will be next month. Now go have a good evening at the hospital," he says with a smile. Abby walks out of his office with a huge smile.

Chapter 16

Monday March 6, 1939.

PEDATRICS, is written across the top of the page. Abby smiles and stares up at the ceiling for a few moments. Mr. Charles asks her if she is alright, and Abby replies that she is fine just a little tired. He looks at his watch and tells her she has four hours to complete the exam, he pauses, smiles and says he will check on her in an hour. He walks away as Abby begins answering the questions.

Exactly one hour later, Mr. Charles enters the room, and Abby is sitting with her hands folded at her desk. He looks at her, and she smiles.

"Either the tests are getting easier, or I am getting smarter," Abby says with a grin.

"I think you are getting smarter," Mr. Charles replies. He continues. "This exam was made as a fourth-year pediatrics final exam. We were curious to see how you would do. I can't wait to grade your paper. I will see you this afternoon in Dr. Jones' office." He takes the papers from her desk and disappears down the hallway.

Her last class ends, and Abby is chatting with a few of her classmates. Word has gotten out about her taking some special exams, and they want to know what is going on. Not knowing exactly what to tell them, Abby says she was chosen as a guinea pig to see how well the classes are going and how they can be improved. They accept her response, and everyone goes their way. Abby walks slowly to Dr. Jones' office and is greeted by his secretary. Abby and the secretary smile and nod at each other as Abby waits to see Dr. Jones.

Mr. Charles rushes past her, not acknowledging her presence. He doesn't knock but throws open the door, races into the office and slams the door shut. As before, Abby can hear them talking but can't make out what is being said. A few moments later the door opens, and Dr. Jones calls for her to enter. She takes the usual seat and looks carefully at the faces of the men in the room. She recognizes Dr. Jones and Mr. Charles, but there are three other men she has never seen before. The men are all talking to each other as if Abby wasn't in the room. She notices the teapot on a tray, and brazenly gets up and pours herself a cup. She retakes her seat and sips her tea while the men ignore her and continue their conversation. It is difficult for her to deduce what's going on as two or three of them are talking at the same time. She can tell the entire conversation revolves around her and the exams she has taken.

Dr. Jones stands up smiles at Abby and pours himself a cup of tea. He nods to Abby and sits back behind his desk. He reclines, sips his tea and smiles at Abby. After a few sips, he sits back up gently puts the cup and saucer on his desk and drums his fingers on the desk for a few moments. The other men have not stopped their conversation, and Abby can see by his facial expression that Dr. Jones is starting to get aggravated.

"Enough!" Dr. Jones shouts as he slams his desk with both hands. "This entire experiment was created to not only tell us what she knows, but how we can create a better curriculum. And standing here arguing with one another is getting us nowhere." The room goes silent after Dr. Jones little tirade, and he slowly sits back down. The four men are a little embarrassed by their behavior in front of Abby. Dr. Jones asks Mr. Charles to tell Abby how she did on the pediatrics exam.

"A perfect score," he says softly, looking at the other men and not at Abby.

Dr. Jones stands and walks over to Abby putting his hand on her shoulder. "The problem is not how intelligent this young lady is. The problem is that you men refuse to admit the fact. Now go back to your books and make me a test she cannot pass."

The men drop their heads and slowly walk out of the office one by one. Dr. Jones takes the teacup from Abby and places it back on the tray. He smiles at Abby and sits back down behind his desk. Abby doesn't know what to do or say, so she just sits waiting for Dr. Jones to say something to her. He drums his fingers on the desk for a moment while looking up at the ceiling. He looks Abby directly into the eyes and says, "Somehow I don't think they can create an exam that you won't pass. Keep up the good work. Oh! And when you do graduate, call me. I want you to be my doctor." He smiles and waves for her to go. Abby thanks him for the compliment and as quickly as she is able leaves his office and heads to the nurses' home to clear her head.

Abby is laying on her bed in the nurses' home when there is a knock on her door.

"come in," she shouts out. The door very slowly opens, and a petite extremely thin young girl peeks her head in the doorway. The two girls stare at each other waiting for the other one to say something.

"Can I help you with something?" Abby asks.

"Sister, told me that there was an empty bed in this room; and if you didn't mind a roommate, I could share with you." The girl says as she balls up her left hand and covers it with her right hand covering her mouth. Abby smiles and remembers the first time she spent the night here with Hyacinth as a roommate.

"Hyacinth has recently moved out so her bed is empty. I would be happy to have you as a roommate. My name is Abby."

"Cynthia. My name is Cynthia and this is my first day here. I just transferred here from Bradford," Cynthia says very softly and with an almost frightened tone in her voice. Abby stands and reaches out her hand to shake hands with Cynthia. Cynthia's handshake is as soft and frightened as her voice. Abby grabs Cynthia's hand with both of hers and squeezes hard.

"When you shake someone's hand, do it like you mean it. Not like you're offering them a dead squid," Abby says with a smile. "That's your bed by the window. Make yourself at home. I was just about to go out. My shift starts at 8:00 pm when does yours?"

Cynthia fumbles with some folded papers and drops most of them. She focuses on the one she is still holding. "I start at 8:00 also. I'm supposed to meet a girl named Abigail

Alexis who I think is my shift supervisor." She says in an almost questioning tone.

"Lucky you," Abby says with a laugh in her voice. "I hear she is a real tough one to work for. See you later," Abby says as she collects her things and goes out the door.

Abby goes back to the portal and then to bed to rest before her shift in the London hospital.

Abby arrives at the hospital early to chat with Matron about supervising the new girl. Matron is in a meeting with the hospital administrator, so Abby has to wait. When the administrator leaves, Matron calls Abby into her office and asks her to have a seat. Abby starts by saying, "Late meeting. I hope everything is alright?"

"Everything is fine, nothing to concern yourself with, child," Matron responds, then she continues. "We have a new nurse starting tonight; her name is Cynthia. I am promoting you to shift supervisor, and you will be responsible for training her. I hope you don't mind."

"A little advanced notice would have been nice," Abby says in a sarcastic tone.

"Don't cop an attitude with me, young lady. Now pour me a cup of tea before I die of thirst." Matron says, then smiles. "How are you getting along at medical school? I haven't seen or spoken to you for quite some time."

Abby pours them both a cup of tea and sits down. They have a long pleasant conversation about Abby and her schooling. She tells Matron all about the new tests she is taking, and they are amazed at how well she is doing. Matron smiles and says, "If they only knew the truth about you, my dear." They both chuckle and then there is a faint knock on the door.

Abby smiles and says, "I bet you that's Cynthia." Unaware that Abby has already met Cynthia, Matron says, "A farthing says it's not."

Abby gives her a thumbs up for the bet, and Matron says, "Enter." The door opens slowly and a very thin frightened face appears in the crack of the door. When she sees Abby, a hint of a smile appears on her face as Matron shouts for her to come all the way in and not to waste so much time entering a room. Cynthia enters the room and stands as close to the doorway as she can.

Matron shouts at her. "When a person enters a room, they enter the room. They don't just stand in the doorway. What's wrong with you child?" Cynthia starts to cry and covers her face with her hands. To break the mood, Abby stands and puts out her palm. "I believe you owe me a farthing," she says with a smile. Matron slaps Abby's hand and turns toward Cynthia. Abby puts her hand up and pats Cynthia on the shoulder.

"Why are you here, Cynthia?" Abby asks her.

"I have a letter of introduction to give to the Matron," Cynthia says slowly.

"Well then do it." Matron demands.

Slowly and cautiously Cynthia pulls out a letter and hands it to Matron. Matron glances at the paper and puts it on the pile of papers on her desk. Then she says, "This is Abby, she will be your supervisor. She will be responsible for you; listen to everything she tells you. Do you understand?"

"I…I'm supposed to meet an Abigail Alexis," Cynthia says.

Matron shakes her head and looks up to the ceiling. "Abby is short for Abigail, my dear girl. Now would the two of you leave my office and get to work…NOW!"

The girls leave Matron's office and head to their ward. On the way, Abby comforts Cynthia and explains to her what she has to do this evening.

By the time their shift is over, Cynthia is a little more sure of herself and not so quiet and shy. Abby walks her to the nurses' home, and tells her she will see her at the hospital tomorrow. She waits for Cynthia to go inside and then she goes to the warehouse through the portal and to her home.

Chapter 17

April 17, 1939.

It's been a long time since Abby visited Douglas at the East End, and she misses their conversations. She decides to make the time to go and visit him.

As soon as school lets out, she makes her way straight to the pub.

Emilie is very busy working behind the bar, and even after all this time, they still haven't actually met yet. Every time Douglas tries to introduce them to each other Emilie is racing off somewhere. Abby walks up to the bar and asks Emilie (who is behind the bar) if Douglas is around. Emilie tells her that he isn't feeling well and is spending the day resting in the apartment in the back. Emilie asks Abby if she would like a drink, but Abby says she just came in to talk with Douglas. Emilie is busy with her customers and has no time for people that just want to talk. Before Abby could leave her a message for Douglas, Emilie is at the other end of the bar serving customers. Abby stands thinking for a few minutes and then orders a drink. It takes Emilie about ten minutes to serve Abby, and then it takes Abby another twenty minutes to finish her drink. Abby leaves the pub and walks slowly back towards the warehouse with her head down looking at her feet and not where she is walking. She walks right into Dave who tells her he had some free time and wanted to see London in the spring. Abby is happy to see him, and they go off wandering around the city.

As luck would have it they wind up in front of the restaurant that Lady Ashley's husband owns. Her car is parked in front, and her chauffeur is sitting behind the wheel. He notices Abby and Dave as they approach the car, and he honks the horn to attract their attention. Abby and Dave smile and walk up the driver asking him how he is and how Lady Ashley is doing. He tells them she is fine and that she is inside the restaurant if they want to go in and see her. They look at each other give a "why not" shrug and proceed inside. The maître d' recognizes the two of them and is happy to see them again. He shows them to Lady Ashley's table. Lady Ashley is sitting with a friend, and they are engrossed in conversation. Abby and Dave approach her from behind and she does not see them. The maître d' excuses himself to her and says that she has some uninvited guests that wish to join her.

"Tell them I am busy and do not wish to be disturbed." Lady Ashley says to the maître d'.

"Well I never," Dave says with a snooty tone.

"How dare…" Lady Ashley starts to say while spinning around to see who is speaking to her. She sees Dave and Abby and jumps to her feet and hugs them both.

"You must join us," Lady Ashley says as her friend stands to be introduced.

"Ann Smith, these are my dear friends Dave and Abby Alexis."

As Dave is about to say his last name isn't Alexis Abby elbows him in the ribs to keep quiet. The four of them have a wonderful time chatting until Abby says that she really must be going. She needs to get some rest before her shift at the hospital. Abby and Dave say their goodbyes and leave to two women in the restaurant.

Once outside, Dave tries to tell Abby he was going to say his name is not Alexis. She holds her hand up to pause him and tells him that he is never to contradict her Ladyship. "It's just not done," she says as they walk slowly back to the warehouse.

Dave changes his clothes and leaves for home as Abby goes to get some much-needed rest.

Later that day, Abby arrives at the hospital ten minutes late, and Matron is on the warpath. Matron shouts at Abby about how she is supposed to be training Cynthia and by being late she is giving the wrong impression to everyone on the hospital staff.

Abby doesn't even attempt to explain her tardiness as Matron wouldn't listen to her excuse anyway. As Abby is walking away from Matron she hears Matron shout. "My office as soon as your shift ends. As soon as it ends!"

It was a busy night, and Abby is exhausted. She is walking towards the exit chatting with Cynthia when she hears. "Where are you supposed to be young lady?"

"Matron's office. I totally forgot," she shouts to Cynthia as she races down the hall to Matron's office.

Matron is standing by the door, and slams it shut as soon as Abby steps into the office. Abby's heart is racing, and she is having trouble catching her breath.

"Sit," Matron says, pointing to the chair. She pours herself a cup of tea; "If you would like one help yourself." Matron says pleasantly. Abby is confused, but pours herself a cup and sits facing Matron.

Nothing is said for a few minutes. Then Matron places her saucer on top of her cup, her signal that she is ready to talk.

"You are supposed to be setting a good example for the new girl. Why were you late?" Matron says sternly.

Abby looks down at the floor for a moment, and Matron clears her throat. Abby looks up into Matron's face and begins to tell her about meeting with Lady Ashley and her friend. Their meeting took longer than she expected, and she didn't get enough sleep. She slept late and raced to the hospital as fast as she was able.

"Would Lady Ashley be willing to corroborate your story." Matron asks.

"I don't see why not." Abby replies wondering why Matron would ask such a question.

Matron looks deep into Abby's eyes and shakes her head. "Doctors are allowed to be late, but not nurses. Remember that," Matron says as she looks down and opens a file.

"You still here? You're going to be late for class if you don't get a move on." Matron says without looking up.

Abby thanks Matron for her time and the tea and runs out of the hospital to medical school.

The entire time she is walking to school, Abby is going over in her mind what just happened with Matron. By the time she sits at her seat in the school, she has forgotten about her conversation with Matron and is focusing on the lecture.

A few of her classmates are getting together for some drinks after school, and one of them asks Abby if she would like to join them. Abby finds this strange as she has always been treated as the black sheep and no one wanted to associate with her before. She thinks for a moment and says she could join them for a short time. Robin her classmate suggests a pub called The East End. He says he heard they have a quaint atmosphere and decent prices for starving medical students. Abby smiles and can't believe her luck. She thinks as they are walking to the pub that she can have a drink excuse herself and head right to the portal next door.

Their small group enters the pub, and Abby is happy to see Douglas behind the bar. Before he says anything to her, she puts her finger to her lips. Douglas winks at her as he recognizes the be quiet signal from Abby. There are six in their group, and they sit at the tables by the front window. Emilie takes their orders and serves them their drinks. The entire time they are sitting there all five of her classmates are asking Abby questions pertaining to the special tests she took. Getting tired of all the questions Abby jumps to her feet and slams the table, getting everyone in the pub's attention. She shouts. "If you want to know about the exams, ask Dr. Jones." She hurriedly grabs her things and races out of the pub to the warehouse. She goes into her house slamming the door from the garage to the house. She screams, and slumps down on her father's chair.

Chapter 18

June 19, 1939.

Abby received a note from Matron to go to the school right after her shift. She enters the medical school and is told to go directly to Dr. Jones office. She can't imagine what's wrong. She took all the exams and passed with the best grades anyone has ever achieved. When she arrives at his office, there is a que of students lined up to see him. She looks at the clock and thinks. "I'm going to be late; please hurry." Her turn finally arrives, and she takes another look at the clock. Five minutes late and she hasn't even started her meeting. Abby walks into the office and is asked to sit down. Dr. Jones tells her that the staff of the medical school is so impressed with her that they have created one last exam for her. He goes on to say that if she does well enough on her exams she will be able to begin her internship in January. Abby is so shocked she is speechless. Dr. Jones continues, "There are five exams, each one lasting approximately seven hours. There will be a fifteen minutes break after three hours, and the first exam will start in thirty minutes. Do you have any questions?"

Abby thinks for a moment and says she has no questions.

"Then get started my dear. Tempus fugit." He says with a smile.

Abby's fifteen-minute break is much needed as she races down the hall to the restroom. She splashes some water in her face and walks to the cafeteria for a snack. A few of her friends ask her where she has been, and she tells them she's taking an exam and she has to get back right away.

Abby takes her seat and continues with her exams. Every fifteen-minute break, she runs to the ladies and grabs a light snack before racing back to the exam room. When she is finally finished she is exhausted. Both mentally and physically. Dr. Gotlieb has been watching her for the last portion of her exam and pats her shoulder when he picks up the papers. He smiles and leaves the room. Abby sits for a few minutes and then slowly gathers herself for a slow walk to the portal and home. She sits on her father's chair and falls asleep.

Chapter 19

July 19, 1939.

Abby has been working so many hours between medical school and two nursing jobs she is becoming burned out. Dave came over the other day to help her with some yard work, and she spent the entire time he was with her, complaining to him and being totally rude whenever he asked her what was wrong. She decides she needs to take a day off, but has to ask Matron for permission to take a day. As she is leaving the hospital at the end of her shift, she leaves a note on Matron's desk that she would like to speak with her. Saturday the twenty-second is the day she would like off, and as she enters the hospital on the twentieth, Matron sees her and calls her into her office.

"I saw your note. What seems to be the problem?" Matron asks her as soon as Abby enters her office.

"I was wondering if it would be at all possible to have this Saturday off," Abby asks with a hesitant almost frightened tone in her voice.

Matron sits and taps her fingers on her desk for a few moments. She is staring intently into Abby's eyes. Abby is standing at attention and is very uneasy. She can't seem to stand still and is wondering what to say next. Matron stops tapping leans forward and says, "Why?"

"May I please sit down?" Abby asks.

"If you must, but again, why do you need the day off?" Matron says with no emotion in her tone.

Abby sits up straight and without thinking simply blurts out, "I just need a day off. I am stressed out and totally exhausted."

There is a long period of silence as Matron ponders Abby's request. Matron stands and pours herself a cup of tea. Abby has learned from experience that when Matron starts a cup of tea she doesn't proceed with a conversation until she finishes and places the saucer on top of the cup. Abby rises from her seat and pours herself a cup without asking for permission. Matron is staring out the window and not paying attention to Abby. Matron is very slowly sipping her tea, and Abby has finished hers first.

Matron places the saucer on top of the cup and looks deep into Abby's eyes. "What do you do in your other life my dear?" Matron asks.

Abby slowly responds, "I am a nurse in the maternity unit of the local hospital. I work part-time so that I can spend more time here and attend medical school. When I am home and not at work, I spend all my time studying."

Matron slowly smiles a slight smile. She rises from her chair, closes the door and the blinds on the door window. She retakes her seat and says, "I am so proud of you. I am not in a position to show you my joy, but deep down inside I am so happy that my child turned out so well without my guidance. I asked you to never mention that I am your mother, and you have kept my wishes. I ask you to never mention that fact to anyone. I will do all I can to help you further your career, but I can never be your mother or your friend. When you become a doctor, and I know you will. I will be working for you. That would make me happier than you can ever know."

Abby is confused. All she asked for was one day off, and Matron is getting deep and philosophical with her. She doesn't say anything but looks at the time. It is late, and she should be starting her shift. Matron rises again and holds her arms out. The two women embrace for what Abby views as a very uncomfortable hug. Matron releases her smiles again and says, "You may have the day off. Now get to work; you are late."

Abby thanks Matron and races out of the office and to her ward to start work.

When Abby's shift ends, Cynthia is walking out of the hospital with her. Cynthia has not made many friends since she has been here and is hoping Abby would be one of them. She asks Abby if she would like to spend some time together today. Abby tells her she has to go to school. Even though it is summer and technically there is no school, Abby tells Cynthia that she signed up for summer classes to learn as much as she can. The two women walk to the nurses' home together, and while Abby is changing her clothes, they have a pleasant conversation. Abby asks Cynthia if she is working this Saturday and is happy to hear that she isn't. Abby tells her that she has the day off, and they will spend the day together. As she is about to leave, Abby says, "Think of something for us to do on Saturday." Abby closes the door and races off to school.

After breakfast, Cynthia spends her morning thinking about what she would like to do on Saturday.

Saturday morning.

Abby and Cynthia are getting dressed to go out. Abby tells Cynthia that they need to make a quick stop before they do anything else. Abby takes Cynthia to the now closed food kitchen she had started. Abby puts the kettle on to make one last pot of tea before leaving the food kitchen. The landlord is due to meet them in about a half an hour, and

Abby wanted to arrive early for one last look around. As the kettle starts to sing, Abby's eyes swell with tears. She is sad to close down the at one time much needed place for a hot meal and neighborhood companionship. Cynthia tells Abby to stay seated while she goes to make them their tea. Just as she is about to pour the second cup, a few people walk in asking if they are reopening. Sadly, Abby tells them that they are closed for good, but they are more than welcome to join her and Cynthia for a cup of tea. They all sit down with their cups held high and toast Abby's soup kitchen. As they reminisce of times past, the landlord arrives to take the keys from Abby. Someone offers him a cup of tea. He joins the group sipping their tea; and when the tea is finished, they start to clean up.

As their guests slowly depart, Abby and the landlord have a private conversation in the corner. Cynthia finishes the last of the washing up, giving Abby and the Landlord their space. When she ends her conversation, Abby motions to Cynthia and they walk out of the soup kitchen together, leaving the landlord to lockup.

The two women walk slowly along the pavement until they reach the entrance of the East End. Abby urges

Cynthia to go inside for a drink. Cynthia hesitates for a moment then smiles and follows Abby into the pub.

The East End is slow as they enter, and Douglas is happy to see Abby again. As soon as he sees her, Douglas fills a glass and places it in front of Abby. Before acknowledging the drink, Abby introduces Cynthia to Douglas; and as Cynthia raises her hand to shake hands, Douglas places a drink in in her hand. Douglas pours himself a half pint, and the three of them toast; "to good times ahead."

After about fifteen minutes of chatting and drinking, Cynthia excuses herself to go to the ladies. Douglas leans in close to Abby and asks her if she can do him a favor. Abby smiles and tells him she will be happy to. Douglas asks her to get him some racetrack winners because business has been slow, and he is a little short on his finances. Abby laughs and says she will have him fixed up in a couple of days.

They clink their glasses and smile at each other. Cynthia comes back to the bar as Abby is finishing her last sip. Abby thanks Douglas for the drinks, and the two women go on their way.

Cynthia suggests they go to a movie, but Abby is not in the mood. They slowly walk past the theatre, and Cynthia tugs Abby's arm pulling her towards the ticket window. Abby gives in and they go into the theatre for the early show.

They find seats in the middle of the theatre, and a few moments after they sit down four men sit behind them. They don't notice the men at first, but as soon as the first reel starts, the men start trying to get the women's attention. Abby and Cynthia ignore the men at first, but soon the men jump over the seats and are now sitting beside the two women. Two men on either side of them. Abby and Cynthia are trying to ignore the men, but the men are acting childish and will not leave the women alone. The women tell the men multiple times to leave them alone, but the men become more obnoxious. The men directly next to the women put their arm around them and attempt to kiss them. Cynthia jumps to her feet and screams as loud as she can for the police. As it happens, an off-duty officer is in the theatre and jumps to his feet after hearing the scream for help.

"Officer Bobby Doyle, Miss. Is there some way I can be of service?"

"These men won't leave us alone," Cynthia shouts to Bobby.

The men start to get up and head for the aisle when some patrons stop them and hold them.

"Would you like to press charges, Miss." Bobby asks.

"We just want to be left alone." Abby says.

Abby grabs Cynthia's hand and starts to pull her towards the exit.

As they exit the row and are in the aisle, Cynthia asks Bobby to hold the men for a few minutes so they can leave the theatre and not be followed. Bobby agrees, and the women walk as fast as they can to the East End.

A couple of drinks later, they have stopped shaking and feel relaxed. The pub is still a little slow, and Douglas joins them for a chat. He asks them if they would like another round, and they both say "No thank you." Douglas stands and starts to collect the empty glasses as Bobby walks in. Bobby asks the women if they are alright, and they tell him they are fine. Cynthia goes to the ladies, and Douglas asks Abby if she could get him some racing results. She smiles and tells him that he already asked her earlier.

Abby asks Bobby to walk Cynthia back to the Nurses' housing because she has to take care of some business by herself. Cynthia comes back to the table and Abby explains to her that Bobby will walk her back home as she has something to do. The women hug and say goodbye. Cynthia leaves with Bobby, and Abby gets a goodbye hug from Douglas. Abby goes through the portal and relaxes on her father's chair.

Chapter 20

August 1, 2019.

Abby awakes to the sound of her phone ringing. She answers and is happy to hear from her old friend Samantha. Samantha asks Abby if she would be able to come to her wedding. Realizing its short notice, Samantha understands if Abby can't make it. Abby asks when the wedding will be and Samantha tells her it's next week, August 10. Samantha continues to tell Abby the wedding will be at her fiancé's home in Saskatchewan Canada. Abby tells Samantha that she will need to check on a few things and get back to her tomorrow. They chat for a few more minutes and say goodbye. Abby slowly gets out of bed and starts to get herself ready for her day.

While sipping her coffee and glancing at the morning paper, there is a knock on the front door. Abby is happy to see Dave arrive early. She had asked him to come by and do a little plumbing repair for her. She was having an issue with her shower faucet dripping. She offers him a cup of coffee before he starts, and he is glad to accept.

After the repair is completed, Abby tells Dave about the wedding invitation. She tells him that she needs a plus one and asks him if he knows anyone who wants to go to Canada for a couple of days next week. He laughs and says he doesn't know anyone; but if it's okay with Emily, he would be glad to help her out. He goes on to say that he has never been to Canada and would like to cross it off his list. Abby points to the telephone, and Dave calls Emily. He explains about the wedding and then is silent for a few minutes. He hangs up the phone turns to Abby and says, "She says to have a good time."

Abby jumps out of her seat and gives Dave a big hug.

"You're a life-saver," she says. She pauses for a moment and releases her grasp. She smiles and asks Dave if he would like to take a short jaunt into the past.

He says, "I thought you'd never ask."

They both let out a little laugh and proceed to the garage to get ready to go.

The time flies by quickly, and Abby and Dave are at the airport waiting for their flight to board. While they are sitting and staring at the departures screen, a woman in the distance catches his eye. Dave gives Abby a little nudge and points out the woman that grabbed his attention.

"Is that Emily?" Abby asks.

"No, Emily took the kids to her parents for a few days. She looks just like you though. Could be your twin sister." He says.

"If I had a twin sister. I'm an only child as far as I know," Abby responds.

They take their eyes towards the departures screen; and when they look back towards the woman, she is gone. They look at each other and at the same time say, "Could there be a portal in the airport?" They pause for a moment and then they both let out a laugh. They smile and take their gaze towards the departures screen again. Sitting in silence for a few minutes, Abby jumps to her feet and says she wants to go see if there is a portal in the airport. She grabs Dave by the hand, and they walk briskly to where the woman they were looking at was standing. They turn the corner and the terminal ends. There is no gate on this side and only a few seats. There is a wall to their right and windows in front of them and to their left. There is no place the woman could have gone. Dave laughs and starts to hum the theme to the Twilight Zone. Abby hands her bags to Dave and asks him to wait for a moment. She walks slowly rubbing her hand along the wall trying to find a portal. Abby is at the end of the wall when her hand passes through it. Her face lights up as she turns to Dave and shouts, "Eureka!" She puts her hand over mouth and walks back to Dave. Just as she picks up her bags the announcement is made for their flight to board.

"When we return," Dave says as they walk to their gate.

It's a long drive from the airport to the small-town where Samantha lives. The travelers are tired and hungry when they arrive. There is only one hotel in town, and it is also a bar and restaurant. Abby goes to the desk to check in as Dave looks over the menu for the restaurant. Dave is not paying attention to Abby and is startled when she shouts out, "That won't do!"

He walks over to her; and before he says anything, Abby shouts at Dave that there is only one room left, and they will have to not only share a room, but also a bed. Dave tells her to calm down and finish checking in. They will sort it all out after dinner. On the way to the room, Abby doesn't stop complaining about the situation. The more she talks about it, the angrier she becomes. Once inside the room, Dave plops their bags on the bed and looks around. There is one queen size bed and a loveseat in the room. Dave tells Abby that she should take the bed, and he will sleep on the loveseat. He pushes her to the door, and they go to the restaurant for dinner.

While they are waiting for their food to arrive, they can't help but hear the conversations going on around them. Everyone is talking about the big meeting tonight. When the waitress brings them their food, Abby asks about the big meeting tonight. She tells them that the city is in dire straits and has no money. They raised the taxes recently but there just isn't enough income to cover all the expenses.

As their table is being cleared, Abby and Dave rise to exit the restaurant. The waitress asks them to sit in on the meeting.

"A different perspective may help," she says.

They sit back down as the room fills. The mayor calls the meeting to order, and it takes many gavel bangs to get the room to quiet down. After everyone has said their piece, the mayor opens the floor for anyone who may have an idea on how to raise enough income to not only cover the present expenses, but future expenses as well. Abby (timidly) raises her hand. The mayor points at her, and she stands to speak.

"Why don't you put in an offer to host the Olympics. The federal government will pay all the bills and the city will make money." She says and then quickly sits back down.

Then looking directly at Abby, the Mayor asks if anyone has any real suggestions. Abby sinks into her chair feeling all eyes in the room on her. The meeting ends without any resolution to the financial crisis.

Walking back to their room, Dave informs Abby that every country that hosts the Olympics loses Billions of dollars. Abby tells him it was just a suggestion. They look at each other and let a little laugh.

"Wasn't that wonderful," Abby says as they walk slowly back to their room following the wedding reception. "I lost count of how many times I was asked when we were going to tie the knot.

"About as many times as I was," Dave responds. Then continues. "I can't wait to get home and sleep in a real bed. Sleeping on this loveseat is ruining by back."

Abby asks him if he would like to share the bed if he promises not to tell anybody. He thinks for a moment and responds that that would not be a good idea.

"The loveseat can suffice for one more night," he says with a slightly pained expression.

The morning is busy with packing, dressing and washing up. Samantha and her new husband Andy offered to drive them back to the airport. Abby and Samantha are chatting during the entire ride. Andy and Dave barely say a sentence each during the trip. They arrive at the terminal and say their goodbyes with plenty of time to spare before their flight home.

Abby is very quiet during the flight home and can't seem to sit still. After a few hours, Dave asks her why she is so fidgety. Abby whispers that she can't wait to check out the portal in the airport. She has been dying to see where it leads.

Upon exiting the gate in the terminal, Abby walks as fast as she can towards where she found the portal. She leaves Dave with their bags, and he is following at a slower pace. While passing a series of lockers, Dave pauses and places the bags in one of the lockers. By the time he catches up to Abby, she is at the wall where she found the portal. She is waiting for him to catch up with her so they can go through the portal together. They take hold of each other's hand and proceed through the portal.

Abby and Dave find themselves on a street in what appears to be New York City at the turn of the century. There is no one around, and it is very quiet. They walk to the end of the street and then back to where they started. The stores are all empty, and all of the apartments appear to be empty as well. Dave walks up a small flight of stairs and attempts to open the door of an apartment building. The door opens easily, and Dave lets out a laugh. Abby is confused, and Dave motions for her to come to see inside. Abby looks inside the doorway and lets out a laugh. They look at each other and together say aloud "It's a movie set." A small part of their quandary has been answered. They kind of know where they are, but WHEN is the big question. They continue walking down the street and are walking through an old western town. They hear noise coming from a short distance away, and they slowly walk towards the sounds they are hearing. They turn a corner and are now on a street that appears the be in the late 1940s. There are people all around with lights and cars and even a fire engine. There is a table with food set up, and Dave nudges Abby to go towards the food table for a snack. As they fill their plates with sandwiches and fruit, a man comes over to them yelling at them.

"Why aren't you in costume? We're behind schedule as it is. Wardrobe!"

Abby and Dave don't get to eat their snack as they are forced into a nearby building. It's a small warehouse filled with clothing and accessories. There is a small desk near the door with some papers on it. Dave glances at the papers and sees the date is 1949. A voice is heard shouting into the warehouse, "Are they ready yet?"

"Almost," a woman helping Abby pick out shoes shouts back.

Abby and Dave look at each other and are giddy with excitement. As soon as they are out the door, a man pushes them to a location on the street. They are given directions on what to do and ordered not to speak out loud, "Just mime the words," they are told sternly. They are told to walk towards an X on the pavement and get into the taxi cab when the principal actors exit it.

The scene is filmed six times with different results each time. The director is visibly unhappy with the scene and shouts to do it again. Dave and Abby start their walk a few moments early. The taxi cab pulls up to them, and the door flies open knocking Abby to the ground. No one yells "CUT" so they continue as if that was supposed to happen. Dave helps Abby to her feet, and the leading man Orson Green asks her if she is alright. Abby tells him she is fine, and he helps her into the taxi with Orson in his way Dave cannot get into the car, so he walks around and enters from the other side. The car drives about a half a block, and they hear "CUT!"

The two of them can't seem to stop laughing about what is going on.

"Hope it's a comedy." Dave says as they exit the taxi and look towards the director to see what to do next. There is a big discussion going on around the director, and Abby wants to get closer to hear what is going on. Dave heads towards the food and Abby near the director. He looks her right into the eyes and shouts at her, "Who said you could talk?"

Without thinking she snaps back, "Common decency."

Then Orson Green taps Abby on the shoulder and asks her if she is okay. He offers her a cigarette, and she refuses. She tells him she is fine. Just a couple of bruises. The big conversation seems to be winding down and someone shouts out, "That's a wrap the filming for today is done return tomorrow at stage three if you're in the nightclub scene."

Abby is walking towards Dave who is near where the food was, but the table is now empty. A man jogs up to them and asks them for their agent's name. A little confused, they ask why only to find out that the director likes their look and wants them for the nightclub scene tomorrow. He lowers his voice to a whisper and says they will both have speaking parts. Abby puts out her hand to shake the man's hand and tells him that she is their agent.

"I am Abigail Alexis and this is David Ivanovitch. What time tomorrow would you like us here?"

He tells her setup starts at six in the morning, but they need to arrive in makeup at seven. They shake hands, and he wanders off as Abby and Dave go back to the warehouse to change into their own clothes. Abby keeps the shoes hoping no one will notice. They hang around the outside of the building and (when no one is looking) they walk off towards the portal.

Back in the airport, Dave gets their bags from the locker. While walking to the exit, Abby keeps talking. She is so excited.

"I told you that was him. You said it wasn't, but I knew it was him. We are going to be in a film with Orson Green. He even offered me a cigarette. I wonder if I should ask him for his autograph tomorrow?"

The entire drive home Abby is just non-stop talking about them being in a Hollywood movie. He pulls the car into her driveway and asks what time she wants him to pick her up tomorrow. First she says three then four then five.

"I'll pick you up at five. That should give us enough time to get to stage three by seven." Dave says as Abby exits his car.

As Dave is driving home, he is trying to figure out what to say to Emily to leave the house at four thirty in the morning. He has no idea what he is going to say as he pulls the car into the garage. Once inside the house, he realizes that Emily took the kids to her parent's house, and she won't be home for a week and a half.

August 13, 2019

Dave arrives at Abby's house at 4:45 in the morning. He knocks on the door, and she opens it instantly.

"I made some coffee for us before we head out." Abby says as she ushers Dave into the house and to the kitchen. They are both quiet as they sip their coffee when all of a sudden Dave shouts out, "Houston, we have a problem."

"What's wrong?" Abby asks.

Dave tells her that they won't be able to get to the portal without a ticket. Abby puts her hand to her head and thinks for a minute. She goes to her computer and looks up flights departing their airport. She scrolls through the fares and finds a one-way flight for fifty-nine dollars.

Abby says, "We buy two one-way trips for fifty-nine dollars, and don't use them. We go to Hollywood have some fun making a movie and then come home and return the tickets."

Dave smiles sips his coffee and agrees.

Before departing for the airport, Abby suggests they change into their 1939 clothes. "A little less conspicuous," she says. Abby grabs a small suitcase as they exit the house. Dave asks her what the suitcase is for, and Abby says, "souvenirs."

The airport is more crowded than they expected, and they get to the studio back lot later than they planned. By the time they find stage three it is half past seven. They are rushed to makeup, and their wardrobe is waiting for them. When they are finished getting made up, they are led to the set where the night club scene is going to be filmed. Most of the setup is done and there are many people standing and sitting waiting to be told what to do.

Two men start directing people to tables. A few are asked to stand on the dance floor. Abby and Dave are waiting to be told what to do. Everyone is in their position except for Abby and Dave. The director arrives and calls for Abby and Dave by name. While they walk to the director, Dave asks Abby how he could know their names. She says the man they met yesterday must have told him. Dave smiles in agreement. The director tells Abby that they looked over the dailies from yesterday, and the car door knocking her down was a great shot. He goes on to say that they want to use that as a running gag throughout the picture. Abby and Dave look at each other and smile. One of the men who was setting up the scene takes Abby and Dave to their location near a door to the kitchen. They are told what to do and where to stand. Another man and a woman come over to them with some papers and ask them to sign a contract. They both laugh as they sign the papers. The woman asks them for their address and Abby tells her they have no permanent address yet. Abby asks if they could use the studio address in the meantime, and the woman agrees. Someone yells out "Places. This is a run through." Then Orson Green and Matilda Silver, the leading actress, walk slowly to the center of the dance floor. They share some dialog that Abby and Dave cannot hear. Matilda runs off and goes through the kitchen door with Orson following. There is some conversation around the director, and some of the extras are asked to move to other locations. Abby turns to Dave and says she is relieved. She thought the door was going to hit her. A voice is heard shouting, "This is a take. Everyone to one." Abby stands where she was told, and someone comes from the other side of the kitchen door. He places an X on the floor with tape and asks Abby to stand on the X.

Dave laughs and says, "X marks the spot. Start digging for the buried treasure."

Abby slaps him and someone yells, "Action." Orson and Matilda start in the middle of the dance floor, and - like before - she storms off through the kitchen door. The door swings, and Orson pushes it wider and slams the door into Abby, knocking her to the floor. Dave reaches to help her up as Orson steps in front of him with his hand out.

"We really need to stop meeting like this," he says as he helps her to her feet. Abby looks at Dave who is smiling and shaking his head. A couple of crew members come over and ask Abby if she is hurt, and she says, "Only my pride." They help her to a seat and offer her some water. Dave is still smiling and shaking his head.

"What," Abby says to him.

"I never thought you would be one of the 'Three Stooges." Dave answers back to her.

They both pause for a moment then Abby blurts out, "Moe, Larry, Curly and Abby." The people near them hear this, and a chuckle is heard from most of them. The man that offered Abby the water comes back and asks her if she is ready to go again. Her eyes light up and she shouts out, "Again!"

"Back to one," is heard, and Abby slowly sets herself on her X.

Dave laughs and says, "Welcome to show business."

The same scene is done four more times. Abby is starting to get bruises from being struck by the door and falling. A long conversation is being held around the director.

Someone yells out. "That's a wrap," and most of the people start to exit the stage. Abby is bruised and tired. She tells Dave she just wants to sit and relax for a few minutes. The director comes over and sits across from Abby.

"You were wonderful, you're first take was the best," he says to her. Abby jumps out of her chair, shouting at him.

"You made me do that five times when all I needed to do was one!"

He calmly says," That's the biz. You get a day off tomorrow, but we will need you for the next three days after that."

She sits back down and looks at Dave for help, support or advice. Dave just smiles, shakes his head and says, "that's the biz, Abby."

"You are absolutely no help what-so-ever," she says sternly.

The director stands (and as he walks away) he turns to Abby and Dave and says, "You two are doing better than I expected. I'm going to see to it you get an increase in your pay."

Dave turns to Abby and asks her if she is ready to go home. She stares at him for a moment and says, "I could really go for a long hot bath."

On their way back to the New York street portal. Abby stops in the wardrobe building. She calls out and there is no answer back. She opens her suitcase and stuffs a few items into it. She smiles at Dave and says, "souvenirs."

"That's not right." Dave says. Abby pouts and places a ten pound note on the small table by the door.

"Happy now?" she says with grin.

Dave makes a face and shakes his head in disapproval. Abby walks swiftly towards the portal and Dave jogs to catch up with her.

Minutes after Dave drops Abby off at her house, she slips into a nice hot bubble bath.

August 15, 2019

Dave arrives at Abby's house at 4:00 am to pick her up for their trip to Hollywood. Abby's face has some bruises from the other day of filming.

"I don't know how much more of this I can take," she says as she gets into his car.

"Did you get the tickets?" He asks.

"I forgot. I'm sorry. I had to work and was too busy," she answers as she is about to exit the car and go back into the house. Dave stops her and tells her that he thought as much, so he purchased them. Abby thanks him and stares out the window. The entire drive to the airport Abby is uncharacteristically quiet. Dave asks her a few times if she is okay. She keeps saying she is fine. "Just tired." They go through the portal and look at each other. At the same time they both ask, "Where are we supposed to go?" After a slight laugh they decide to find the main entrance. The closer they get to the main entrance the more crowded the studio becomes. As they are approaching the main gate, a voice calls out from behind them calling out their names. They turn and see the man they gave their names to the first day they were here. Dave waves and Abby grabs his arm. She feels faint and needs to hold him to keep her balance. The man sees her almost fall and rushes to her. With a man on each arm, Abby slowly walks to the infirmary. After a quick check-up, it is determined she is just lacking food and hydration. The nurse asks her when the last time she ate and Abby thinks for a moment. The nurse (looking directly into her eyes) says, "If you don't eat you will pass out." The nurse gets some food for her as Dave goes to find out where they are supposed to be for filming.

Feeling better after filling her stomach, Dave and Abby head to the sound stage for the days shoot. Because of the detour to the infirmary, the shoot has been delayed. Abby and Dave are rushed through make-up and wardrobe. The set appears to be the lobby of a hotel. People are being placed around the set, and a man comes over to Dave and asks him to stand about ten feet away from a revolving door. Abby is led to the other side of the door. What would be outside if there was an outside. Abby is told she is to be walking down the street in front of the hotel. When she gets to the revolving door, Orson is going to arrive at the same time. They are to both enter the door and collide with each other. Dave is told to run to the door as soon as that happens. Abby smiles and says, "Thank goodness there's no getting hit in the face this time." No one seems to pay her any attention as a shout to go to one is heard. Everyone is in position and "Action" is shouted. As Abby and Orson are about to reach the door, he steps on her foot and she starts to fall towards the door. He tries to catch her, and the two of them fall to the floor and are both hit with the revolving door. Rushing towards them, Dave slips and falls crashing into the door from the inside. There is a moment of silence as no one is quite sure what to do next. Finally "Cut" is called out, and there is a discussion around the director. Orson helps Abby to her feet and apologizes for stepping on her foot. Abby smiles and asks him if now would be a bad time to ask for his autograph. The two of them laugh, and he signs a picture she pulls out of her purse. The director tells them that he doubts they would be able to do that scene any better and for everyone to set up for the next scene inside the hotel lobby. While the assistants are placing the extras for the scene, the director and the lead actors are in a deep discussion. Orson shouts out "I love it," and Matilda smiles. Orson goes to Abby and is having a discussion that Dave cannot hear. Matilda calls to Dave and asks him to sit with her so she can explain what they are going to be doing. Dave smiles and he and Matilda go to a corner to chat some more. Orson asks Abby if her husband will mind the change in the scene. Abby laughs and tells him that Dave is not her husband just a dear friend. She tells him she is not nor has ever been married. He smiles and places his hand on her leg. He whispers that they should get to know each other better. He asks her to come home with him after filming has stopped. Abby tells him she is flattered by the offer, but has to work and will have to take a rain check. He is becoming more persistent and is making her extremely uncomfortable. Dave and Matilda come back from where they were chatting, and Abby calls to Dave. Abby tells Dave that Orson is hitting on her, and she is very uncomfortable being alone with him. She asks Dave to stay as close as he can at all times. Dave agrees, and they sit on a sofa awaiting orders.

A few more scenes of Orson and Matilda are shot, and Abby and Dave are getting bored. The day is dragging on, and Abby has to work again tonight. She tells Dave she hopes this ends soon, she wants to take a nap before work. About a half an hour later, "It's a wrap" is shouted, and everyone starts to exit. Orson, Matilda and the director come over to Abby and Dave for a discussion about what they are going to be doing next. It's a large sofa and Orson sits next to Abby. Matilda sits so close to Dave he doubts he could slide a dollar bill between them. The director calls for a chair, and someone brings one over for him. The discussion is going on and on. Every time Dave glances towards

Matilda she winks and smiles at him. Now he is getting as uncomfortable as Abby is with Orson. The conversation ends and the four actors stand up. Orson grabs Dave by the arm and pulls him away from the women.

"I have a car waiting at the studio exit. The four of us are going out for dinner and then (he winks) we'll see what happens," he says to Dave.

Dave doesn't say anything to Orson, he just takes Abby by the arm and they go to change their clothes. Abby peeks out the door of their dressing room and no one is around. As fast as they can, they run to the portal and are back in the airport. As soon as they appear in the airport terminal, a small boy sees them and starts shouting, "Ghosts! Ghosts!"

Dave tries to calm the boy down, but with no success. Abby grabs Dave's arm, and they walk briskly to the airport exit.

On the drive back to her house, Abby tells Dave she doesn't want to go back and finish the movie. She is so disappointed with Orson's behavior. Dave tries to explain to her that that is how Hollywood was back then. He promises he will keep an eye on her the entire time they are in the studio. Reluctantly, Abby agrees to continue with the movie.

Dave arrives at Abby's house at 4:00 am. He knocks repeatedly but receives no answer. He walks around to the garage entrance and uses the key Abby gave him to open the garage door. He shouts for Abby, but he gets no response. He walks around the house and then sits at the kitchen table for a few minutes. Suddenly, Abby appears in the doorway from the garage. She looks tired and drowsy. Dave asks her if she is alright? She tells him it was a rough night at the hospital in 1939. He tells her she can nap in the car on the way to the airport.

Once through the portal and in the back lot, they find their way to stage three. After makeup and wardrobe, Abby and Dave are brought to the night club set. Extras are being placed around the set and Abby and Dave are shown two X's on the floor. They are told that this will be their mark for starting the scene. They are taken to a couple of chairs placed by the director. Orson and Matilda are sitting there and are ignoring Abby and Dave. Abby says hello to the two of them but gets no response. She turns to Dave and says, "Brr can you feel the cold shoulder."

Dave chuckles and whispers to Abby, "They must be mad because we ditched them last night."

Matilda gets off her chair and asks Abby to sit in hers. Matilda sits next to Dave and asks him why they didn't show last night. Dave tells her that it is kind of embarrassing. Matilda pressures him, and Dave tells her that after he and Abby changed into their street clothes he had a sudden attack and had a terrible mess in his trousers. Abby put her hand in front of her face and tried as hard as she could to hold back the laughter. Matilda put her hand on Dave's arm and asks if he is feeling better today.

Dave says, "A little."

Before any more is said on the subject, a shout to one comes from behind them. Orson stands and helps Abby from her chair. He seems to be a little more pleasant since hearing about Dave's trouser disaster. He takes Abby by the hand and leads her to her starting mark. Matilda puts her hand out for Dave to help her up and they proceed to their marks. The assistant director shouts out to everyone what is about to happen and then someone else shouts out, "This is a rehearsal." The scene unfolds with Orson and Matilda dancing in the middle of the dance floor. Abby and Dave are dancing about twenty feet away from them. After a couple minutes of dancing, Orson and Matilda are next to Abby and Dave. A waiter carrying a large tray of dishes is trying to get between them. Orson spins Matilda into the waiter who crashes into Abby sending the tray and dishes crashing on

Abby's head. Luckily for Abby, the tray and dishes were rubber props and didn't hurt her. "Cut," is yelled out and then, "Back to one." Everyone goes to their starting spot and "This is a take," is shouted out.

The music starts, and the dancers are dancing. Orson and Matilda move next to Abby and Dave as the waiter is trying to get passed them. Orson spins Matilda who crashes into Dave instead of the waiter. Dave slips and trips the waiter who drops the tray on Orson. Abby starts to laugh as "Cut," is shouted out.

A long discussion takes place around the director. Everyone not in on the discussion is standing around waiting to hear what to do next. The director walks over to Abby, Dave, Orson and Matilda. Orson and Matilda are smoking, and Abby is trying not to inhale the smoke. The director says the shot was perfect, and they are going to pick up exactly where they left off.

It takes about twenty minutes for everyone to get in the exact position where they should be. Dave and Orson are on the floor with the tray and dishes. Abby is holding Matilda as she caught her after she collided with Dave. "Action" is shouted and Abby pushes Matilda away to get to Dave on the floor. Orson looks up at Abby and says that if they are going to continue meeting like this they should at least introduce themselves to each other. Dave helps Orson up and tells him his name is Dave and introduces Abby to him as Abby. "Cut," is shouted out, and they all stop. The director steps over to them and asks why Dave is using his real name and not his character's. Dave tells him that he and Abby were never given character names. A small discussion is held, and the result is Dave is Dave and Abby is Abby. They position themselves to do the scene again, and the director is happy with the result. Abby, Dave, Matilda and Orson are positioned on the dance floor for the next scene. After that is finished, they are taken to a table for the next shot. Abby and Orson are told to have a conversation and then leave together. Dave and Matilda are left sitting at the table, emptying a bottle of champagne. The film ends with Orson and Abby getting married, Dave is the best man and Matilda is the maid of honor.

Everyone is happy the film is finished, and all the conversation is about the wrap party later. Matilda grabs Dave and tells him he is going to the party and she will not take any excuses. He tells her he needs to check with Abby, and Matilda tells him that Orson is getting Abby to attend. Abby tells Orson that she won't be able to attend because she has to work. He ignores everything she says and calls over a security guard to escort her to his car. Abby is trying to get Dave's attention, but Matilda and the director have him by the arms and are pulling him to the exit. With no escape, Abby and Dave are forced to attend the party. The party is held at the house of the producer of the film in Beverly Hills. There is a large crowd, and all the conversation is about the film and all the times Abby was knocked down. After about twenty minutes, some speeches are given. After the speeches, one of the revelers strips down to her underwear and jumps into the pool. Suddenly clothes are being strewn all over the place as people are stripping down and jumping into the pool. Dave manages to find Abby in a corner with Orson trying to get her to drink something. She is trying to fend him off, but he is being very persistent. Dave walks up to the two of them and whispers in Orson's ear. Orson smiles and jumps to his feet. Dave puts his arm around Orson and leads him about five feet away from Abby. Dave pretends to wave at someone across the pool, and Orson looks to see who he is waving at.

Dave pushes Orson into the pool and rushes to Abby. He grabs her hand, and the two of them run through the house and out of the front door. Orson's car is the nearest one they see, and Dave checks to see if the keys are in the ignition. He shouts for Abby to get in and they drive off.

After driving around for an hour, they realize they are lost. Abby sees a police officer on the side of the road, and Dave pulls over to him. Abby asks the police officer how to get to the studio and he gives them precise directions. She thanks him, and they drive off. It takes them another hour to find the studio, and approach the main entrance slowly. Dave tells the guard that Abby left her purse in stage three and they will only take a few minutes to pick it up. He asks them their names and sees them on the list from the past few days. He lets them in, and they drive straight to the street where the portal is. They go through the portal and are happy to be back in the airport terminal. Abby takes the tickets to the desk to turn them in and is asked to wait a moment. She turns and looks at Dave with a questioning look on her face. He walks to her and asks what's going on. She tells him she doesn't know but was asked to wait. A moment later six police officers surround them and ask Abby and Dave to come with them. They are taken to separate rooms and searched. They are asked many questions about why they keep buying tickets and never using them. Neither of their answers match, and they are held in their rooms for over two hours. Dave is being cocky and giving sarcastic answers to all the questions. Abby is scared and trying to be as honest as possible without saying they are time travelers. With no evidence of illegal activity and nothing further to hold them on, Abby and Dave are released.

The drive home is somber and quiet. When Dave pulls the car into Abby's driveway, Abby sits and stares at the house. Dave is looking down and neither of them is talking.

"Please come in for some coffee. I don't feel like being alone right at this moment." Abby says with a very sad tone in her voice.

"What about your work?" Dave says.

Abby doesn't answer him. She just moves slowly, opening the car door and going into her house. Dave follows her, and neither of them is speaking. Dave sits at the table, and Abby makes them a pot of coffee. She pours each of them a cup and sits at the table across from Dave. Sipping in silence, Abby begins to open up.

"I need a break from Hollywood," she says.

Dave shakes his head in agreement, and nothing more is said until their cups are empty. Dave stands to pour them each another cup when Abby stands and tells him she really should get to work.

"It's better to show up late than not at all," she says.

Dave puts the coffee pot down, gives Abby a hug and a kiss on her cheek. She squeezes him tightly, and he smiles. They separate, and Abby tells him he is a wonderful friend. She asks him to thank Emily for allowing him to go to Canada with her. She smiles at him as he leaves through the garage door. Abby changers her clothes and goes through the portal to 1939 to go to work.

Chapter 21

August 26, 2019

Emily arrives back home with their children. She is so excited she is talking non-stop about the wonderful time they had with her parents. Realizing she has been talking so much and hasn't let Dave say a word, she pauses and asks him how his trip to Canada was. Trying to hold back his excitement he tells her all about the trip and the wedding. Just as he is about to spill the beans about the trip to Hollywood the kids start shouting that daddy is on television. Emily and Dave go to the sitting room where the kids are watching an old movies channel. They were hoping to see the "Three Stooges," but the movie Abby and Dave are in is on. Emily's eyes light up and Dave tries to hide his smile.

"That guy looks just like you," Emily says. "And that woman next to him looks just like Abby."

Emily picks up the remote and pauses the film. The title of the film is displayed on the bottom of the screen. The kids are shouting to start the movie, and Emily presses play. She goes over to the computer to search for the movie. Dave and the kids continue watching it. Emily screams, and Dave goes running into the kitchen to see what's wrong. She is speechless and pointing to the computer monitor. Displayed on the screen is the full cast of the film "I Bumped Into My Love" Under Orson Green and Matilda Silver are Abigail Alexis and David Ivanovitch.

"That's you and Abby." Emily says, "But how?"

Dave doesn't know what to say or how to say it. He babbles incoherently as Emily is searching his name in an actors data base. The only reference with his name is the one picture. There is no other information. All it says is that David Ivanovitch costarred in the picture "I Bumped Into My Love."

Not knowing how to reveal the truth to her, Dave says that it is such a strange coincidence that he would have a doppelganger from the 1940s that not only looks like him but has the same name. Emily is not buying a word of his explanation and is getting angry and suspicious of him.

"Are you having an affair with Abby?" Emily shouts at him with tears in her eyes.

Surprised by her comment, Dave shouts back that the idea has never crossed his mind. He tells her that they are good friends and that's all. To prove his point he dials Abby's number. She doesn't answer and the call goes to voice mail. Dave leaves a message for her to call him as soon as she is able. Emily rounds up the kids and her bags that haven't been unpacked yet.

"We are going back to my parents. When you want to tell me the truth, you can call me there," she says as she takes the kids to her car and drives off with Dave totally confused as to what to say or do next. Dave sits and watches the rest of the movie and then decides to go through the portal to 1939 to clear his head.

Dave is wandering the streets, not paying attention to his surroundings. In the distance, he sees the hospital where Abby works. He decides to take a chance and see if she is there.

Dave walks up to the front desk and asks if Abby Alexis is working today. The receptionist asks him to wait a moment, and she will check and see. After a few minutes, Abby approaches Dave and is happy to see him. She leads him to a staff break room and fixes them each a cup of tea. She tells him it's been a slow night, and she is happy for the break. Dave explains to her the argument he had with Emily and that she took the kids and went back to her parents' house. Abby just sits and listens without saying anything. When he is finished talking, Abby puts her teacup down and stares up at the ceiling for a few minutes. She lowers her head and looks Dave directly in the eyes.

"I guess it was wrong to tell them our real names in Hollywood," she says with a slight smile.

Dave smiles and shakes his head. Suddenly Abby's face lights up.

"We made that movie a few days ago, right?" she says excitedly.

Dave says, "Yes, I think so."

Abby continues to tell him that they can go back to Hollywood, go to the studio office and ask that their names be changed in the film. Dave likes the idea and asks her when they can go. She tells him she still has a few more hours to work. She tells him what time to meet at her house, and Dave goes away happy with their conversation.

Dave is waiting in Abby's garage when she comes through the portal from 1939. She asks him to give her a few minutes to change her clothes, and then they can go the airport portal.

At the airport, they purchase their usual tickets and head to the portal.

Once through the portal and into the back lot, they are approached by a security guard who asks them how they got to this part of the lot. Abby smiles and tells him they need to go to the main office, but always wanted to see the rest of the studio. She puts the charm on thick, and the guard offers to drive them to the office. Once inside the studio main office they ask to see the personal director. They are told where his office is, and they are told to wait outside of it. After almost an hour wait, they are told to go in to see the personal director. Abby asks Dave to let her do the talking as he can get a little hot headed when in a confrontational situation. He just smiles and snaps back at her that he does not. They both giggle as they enter the office. The personal director asks them to sit, and Abby begins to explain the reason for their visit. The man doesn't say anything and listens to what Abby says. When she finishes her explanation, the man excuses himself and asks them to wait until he returns. About a half hour later, the man returns with a small stack of papers. He sits at his desk and looks over the papers. After he puts the papers down he looks at Abby and says. "Abigail Alexis, and what name would you like be known by."

Abby thinks for a. moment and says, "Rose Azalea."

The man thinks for a moment and says, "Your name is Azalea Rose, and you, Sir what do you want to be known as."

Dave thinks for a minute and says, "Dermot Marks."

The man thinks for a moment and writes down both names on the papers in front of him. The man makes a few more notes on the papers and then tells them they need to go see the director of performers down the hall. Abby asks him why, and he says something about the contracts they signed. While they walk to the office, Dave seems worried. He tells Abby that he hopes they aren't in some sort of contract trouble. Abby laughs and tells him that in reality they haven't even been born yet. They both stop walking smile and laugh then continue on their way. When they get to the office of performers they are told to sit and wait.

"Seems like a running theme in this company. Sit and wait." Dave says. Abby doesn't respond, just picks up a trade magazine and thumbs through the pages. After almost an hour of waiting, they are told to go into the office. The man behind the desk isn't looking at them, he just has his face buried in some papers.

"Abigail Alexis and David Ivanovitch." The man says without looking up at them.

"Yes," they both say timidly.

Still without looking at them, he hands them each a piece of paper and asks them to sign their names. Abby asks what this is all about and the man says to them, still without looking at them, "You want to get paid, don't you?"

They sign the papers and hand them back to the man who finally puts down the papers he is examining and looks at them.

"You both signed a multifilm contract, and it appears you only made the one picture. I have a memo from Orson Green's agent that he does not want to work with either of the two of you ever again. I can understand you not wanting to work with him, but the other way around I don't get it." The man says. Before either Abby or Dave can answer, the man says that there is another film starting tomorrow, and they are both obligated to be in it. The producer of "I Bumped Into My Love" is producing that picture and he personally requested the two of you. It seems he saw you shove Orson into the pool and realized then and there you are the ones for his next project. Says here leading man and woman. Not bad after making only one picture."

Abby and Dave are speechless. The man hands them their checks for their first film and tells them that they can cash them at the studio cashier down the hall. Abby and Dave aren't sure what to do next, so they are just sitting waiting for the man to say something.

"You still here? Go cash your checks and have a nice day," the man says.

Abby and Dave look at their checks as they walk to the cashier. Abby shows her check to Dave who exclaims "Wow, four thousand dollars; I only got three thousand."

Abby says she gets more for being abused. They both laugh and go to the cashier to cash their checks.

With their hands full of cash, Abby and Dave are trying to decide what to do next. Abby has a wonderful idea. She tells Dave they can go to a bank and exchange the paper money for silver dollars and silver half dollars. As soon as they walk through the portal, their money will increase by whatever the value of silver is at the time. Dave loves the idea, and they exit the studio to find a bank. A block away from the studio entrance is a bank, and they exchange all their paper for coins. They didn't realize how heavy thousands of dollars worth of coins would be. On the way back to the studio, they find a luggage store and purchase four small suit cases to carry the coins in. Before they leave the studio they check with the gate to make sure they can get back in. By the time they get to the airport terminal, they are exhausted from carrying the cases of coins.

On the way back to Abby's house, they pass a stamp and coin shop. Dave suggests they stop in and see what their coins are worth. The man in the shop asks if they are buying or selling, and Abby says selling. The man asks them to sit at a table in the back of the shop. They only brought 100 Franklin half dollars into the store with them. The man asks to see what they want to sell, and Dave places the one-hundred uncirculated half dollars on the table. The man's eyes just about pop out of their sockets when he sees what they have. The man asks to be excused for a minute, and he goes through a door in the back of the store. The man comes back with another man, and they both look over the coins. They offer Abby and Dave two-thousand dollars for the one hundred coins. Abby had looked up the value on her phone as they were waiting for the man to return. She tells the men they will have to do better than that. Without hesitating, the man says three-thousand but he cannot go any higher. Abby smiles and agrees for the three-thousand, and the transaction is completed. As they are leaving, the man asks them where they found such an amazing find. Abby says her father was a coin collector, and this was a small part of the collection. The man hands her his card and asks her to see him before she tries to sell to anyone else. They all shake hands, and Abby and Dave continue on their way to her house.

Dave drops Abby off and continues to his home. When he arrives, Emily and the children are there. Emily runs to him and hugs him. She apologizes for acting the way she did. She tells him she must have been crazy to think that a man in a movie from 1949 could be him. She goes on to say that when she arrived at her parents she told them about the movie and her web search. She went on their computer and brought up the movie. In the cast is shown Orson Green, Matilda Silver, Azalea Rose and Dermot Marks. She continues to say she must have imagined that it said David Ivanovitch and Abby Alexis. If it did that would mean Dave and Abby were time travelers and everyone knows that time travel is impossible.

Dave smiles, kisses Emily and says, "Of course time travel is impossible. Everyone knows that." He hugs her tightly and winks and smiles at his reflection in a mirror. Emily asks Dave what his plans are for the next few days. He tells her he got a repair job starting tomorrow that could last a week or more. Emily smiles and goes to prepare a snack for the kids.

Chapter 22

August 27, 2019

Dave arrives at Abby's house at four in the morning for their trip to Hollywood. As she is getting into his car, she tells him she really isn't in the mood to make anymore movies. He tells her that they did sign a contract and are obligated.

Abby laughs and tells him "they can try to sue us we won't exist until most of them have passed away."

Dave smiles but doesn't say anything. He is enjoying their time together. He doesn't have many friends, and Abby is like the sister he never had. When they arrive at the desk to purchase their tickets, they are told to wait a moment. Some police arrive and take them to the small rooms they were taken to before.

Dave is feeling in a good mood and snaps at the officer that they really should stop meeting like this. The officer is not amused and gives Dave an extra invasive body search. When he is done searching and finds nothing, Dave asks if he is free to go. The officer is slow to respond and opens the door for Dave to leave. Abby is waiting outside the room and asks him why it took so long. Dave laughs and says the officer was looking for Jimmy Hoffa and got mad because he couldn't find him. They both have a little laugh and decide to purchase tickets from a different airline. Abby says that it doesn't matter what the tickets cost because they are going to exchange them anyway. Dave agrees and off to the portal they go. As they are walking through the terminal, Dave tells Abby that he thinks they are being followed. She asks him if they have time to waste, and he says they are doing okay on time. She whispers for Dave to go to a gift shop, and she will go to the lady's room. When she gets out, he will go to the men's room and she will hang around the gift shop to look for any suspicious people. When he gets out of the men's room, he meets her at the gift shop. She points to two men who seem to be watching them. They make a mad dash for the portal and are gone before the two men get around the corner. When the men get to where the portal is, Abby and Dave are in Hollywood.

The street of the portal is buzzing with activity. People are getting the street ready for filming. There are lights and cables and trucks all over the place. Someone yells at them, and they turn to see who is shouting at them.

"Where did you two come from," a security guard yells at them.

Abby bats her eyes and says, "I am Azalea Rose and this is Dermot Marks we thought this was the set they wanted us on."

The guard checks his papers and tells Abby that they are on the wrong set. They have to go to stage six on the other side of the lot. She apologizes and grabs Dave's hand. Together they go skipping through the back lot to stage six. There is a line of extras waiting to enter stage six. Abby and Dave go to a door marked "Talent." Once inside, they ask where they should go. A woman with a clipboard asks them who they are and Abby tells her. She directs them to a small office to her right. She asks them to wait and someone will be with them shortly. After about fifteen minutes, the producer opens the door and shakes hands with Abby and Dave as he introduces himself. All three of them sit as the producer seems uncomfortable in what he is about to say.

"Damnit," He shouts as he stands and bangs on the desk. "I wanted the two of you for my next two pictures, but it seems Mister Orson Green has more power over the top brass than I do. Your contracts have been cancelled with the buyout clause, and you must leave the studio at once. Go to the cashier in the main office, and she will give you your buyout checks. I'm sorry it didn't work out, but that's the biz."

He shakes their hands again and walks out of the office.

Abby turns to Dave and says, "I didn't want to make anymore movies anyway. At least they are paying us for doing nothing."

Dave shakes his head in agreement, and gives Abby a slight smile. He really wants to continue making movies. They walk to the main office and go to the cashier to pick up their checks. The cashier tells them she can cash their checks for them, and Abby Dave walk away with five thousand dollars each. Dave tells her that they better get to the portal before then get thrown out of the studio.

It's a long quiet walk back to the street where the portal is. The security guard that stopped them earlier asks them to stop as a scene is being shot, and no one is allowed in unless they are directly involved in the scene. Abby and Dave wait anxiously for their chance to get to the portal. Someone yells "Cut", and the security guard steps aside so they can pass. They walk the length of the street like they belong there. As soon as they get to the portal, they go through without checking to see if anyone is watching. All they want to do is get home.

In the airport, they go to the desk and return their tickets. As they are walking towards the exit six police officers surround them.

Abby and Dave are taken to the small rooms they were taken to previously. They are asked many questions and are not in the mood to answer any of them. They are searched and then questioned about the money they have on them. Abby tells the officer that she is a time traveler who goes back in time and robs banks. Dave says that they are really Bonnie and Clyde and are working for the FBI. After two hours of questions and nothing to hold them on, Abby and Dave are released and told never to return to the airport again.

Driving back to Abby's house, Dave is very quiet. Abby takes out some of the money that she was paid and notices "Silver Certificate" printed across the top. She shows it to Dave who tells her that they no longer exchange them for silver, but might be worth a little more than face value depending on the condition of the bill. Nothing more is said about the money or the trips to Hollywood.

Dave drops Abby off at her home and continues on his way to his home. Abby stands in her garage looking over her table of accessories. She places the money in an empty shoebox, places the shoebox on the table and goes into the house to make herself a cup of coffee. Abby takes out her notebook and writes about her adventures in Hollywood. After she finishes writing her notes, she takes a short nap before getting ready to go to work in 1939.

When Abby arrives at the hospital for her shift, she is told that Matron is looking for her. Abby goes to Matron's office and finds the door open and no one around. She enters the office and starts to make two cups of tea. When the tea is ready, Matron appears at the door and gives Abby a slight smile.

"Please sit," Matron says as Abby places Matron's cup of tea on her desk. Matron thanks her for the tea, and the two women sit quietly sipping their hot beverages. Matron finishes her tea and places the saucer on top of the cup, her signal for she is ready to start a conversation. Abby is still sipping her tea, but Matron starts talking to her. She tells Abby how proud she is of Abby's work in the hospital. She is also delighted to hear how well she is doing in medical school.

"Now for the reason I needed to talk with you," Matron says with a slight smile. "We are in desperate need of a surgical nurse in the operating theatre. I looked over the qualifications of all of our nurses, and you are the most qualified. Now I realize how busy you are, between medical school and your other career, but your hours will need to be changed. All of our surgeries are scheduled for the early mornings. At those times where there are no surgeries you will be my assistant. The hospital board has already approved these changes, and we are looking forward to you stepping up to the challenge."

Abby is speechless and almost drops her teacup on the floor. Abby sits and stares at Matron for what seems like hours. In reality more like thirty seconds, but to Abby it seems like hours. Matron stands and stretches out her hands to help Abby from her chair. Abby stands slowly and places her teacup and saucer on the desk. Matron pulls Abby close to her for a hug. Abby is uncomfortable with this intimate moment. Matron always seems so stern and unapproachable. Not the friendly hugging type. Matron whispers into Abby's ear.

"I wish I could tell the world that you are my daughter; but alas, that can never happen. I can't explain to you why, but trust me please never say a word of it to anyone."

They part from their embrace, and Matron goes back to her seat. She tells Abby that she will start in surgery tomorrow, so she does not need to work tonight.

"Go home child and work things out with your other job. I will see you bright and early tomorrow at 6:00 am.

On her way back to the portal, Abby stops at the East End to say hello to Douglas. It has been some time since she has seen him and feels now is as good a time as any. The moment Abby walks through the door Douglas sees her and comes running up to her for a big friendly hug. After he releases her, she smiles and says, "Happy to see you, too." He pours them each a drink and demands she tell him all about what is going on in her life. Abby goes on in detail about her trip to Hollywood, and the movie she acted in. He jokingly tells her that he feels sad he has to wait ten years before he can see the film. He asks her when she thinks they will be able to go to the race track as his cash flow is getting a little low. Abby apologizes for not seeing him more frequently and tells him she has no idea when they will be able to go to the races together. She tells him she will get him some results and drop them off on her way through the portal.

Emilie is walking past them as Abby is speaking and she asks what a portal is. Quick on his feet, Douglas says portal is slang for a tube entrance. Emilie says she never heard that expression before, but is learning something new every day. Emilie stays standing near Douglas and Abby, so their conversation changes to the weather and the prospect of war on the horizon. As they are talking about the possibility of war, Abby and Douglas chuckle as they both know what happens since they are both from the future. Since Emilie is standing so close to them, Abby and Douglas feel they can't carry on their usual conversation. Abby finishes her drink, gives Douglas a hug and a kiss and tells him she will see him in the next day or two. Abby exits the pub and goes home. Douglas gives himself a faceplant and says, "I never introduced you two." Emilie smiles, kisses his forehead and goes behind the bar to work.

After Abby changes her clothes and walks into her kitchen, she sees the light flashing on her answering machine. She lets out a laugh and says to the machine that she thinks she is the only person still using such an antique device. She presses the play button and listens to a message from her supervisor at the hospital. Her supervisor wants Abby to call her as soon as she gets this message. Abby phones the hospital and is told her supervisor is in a meeting but wants to see her as soon as possible.

Abby rushes to the hospital and is waiting in her supervisor's office and wondering what this meeting is all about. Susan, her supervisor, walks in says hello and sits down at her desk. She has a folder in her hand, and as soon as she sits down, she opens the folder and begins to read. After reading for a few minutes, Susan puts the folder on her desk and looks at Abby. Susan doesn't say anything, but Abby can see she is thinking.

"We have a problem, and I am hoping you can help us work it out," Susan says. Abby doesn't say anything but listens intently as Susan continues.

"We are over-staffed in maternity and under-staffed in the OR. I am hoping that you would be willing to switch from maternity to OR to help us.

Abby doesn't say anything out loud, but to herself she thinks, "two different hospitals in two different eras and I am switched to the OR. I must be in some kind of a twilight zone."

Susan tells her she is to report to the OR at 5:00 am tomorrow. She goes on to say that although Abby has been working part-time she now has to work a full five day a week shift Monday through Friday 5:00 am to 1:00 pm. Abby asks if she has any say in where and when she works, and Susan explains that if this wasn't an emergency they wouldn't be having this conversation. Susan tells Abby to go home and come back tomorrow morning. Abby leaves the hospital and drives slowly back home. The entire drive home she is calculating the hours she needs to work and the times she will be able to sleep. When she arrives at home, she takes out some paper and a pencil and starts to draw a graph of her daily routine starting tomorrow.

Her hours in 1939 will be 6:00 am to 3:00 pm. In 2019, she will have to wake up at 12:00 am to leave 2019 to be on time in the hospital in 1939. After she leaves 1939, she will be back home in 2019 around 1:40 am. With a short nap to recharge, she will have to leave her house at 4:30 am to be in the hospital at 5:00 am in 2019. She will need to go to sleep about 4:30 pm in 2019 to get enough rest before starting all over again. She makes a note on the side of her paper.

"What happens when medical school restarts?"

Abby does some cleaning around the house and goes to her computer to lookup regulations for nurses in the 1930s and 1940s. According to the health department regulations, nurses are not allowed to get married or have children. She looks up to the ceiling and says, "That's why Matron can't say she is my mother; we would both be fired."

As she is walking towards the hospital, Abby sees at least six ambulances racing towards the hospital. She picks up her pace and walks as fast as she can. As soon as she enters the hospital, she sees people racing around with patients lining the halls. She grabs an orderly and asks what is going on. He tells her there was a train crash and there are too many injured to count. Abby runs to the OR and is reprimanded by the surgeon for not being earlier. He has just finished scrubbing up and yells at Abby to hurry.

Abby looks at the clock and sees that it is 4:30 pm. The day flew by quickly as there were so many patients to see in the operating room. Mr. Grant, the surgeon, is sitting on a chair next to Abby who is sitting on the floor. The two of them are totally exhausted. He takes out a cigarette and offers one to Abby. She tells him she doesn't smoke but thanks him for the offer. He looks over at her and tells her he doubts any other nurse could have done as well as she did today. He tells her he is proud to have her as his nurse and he will tell Matron she made the right choice. Abby smiles and rests her head against the wall. Mr. Grant slowly rises and tells Abby he will see her in the morning. He walks out, leaving Abby alone on the floor. Too tired to stand up, Abby dozes off.

A hand is gently rocking Abby. She opens her eyes to see Matron trying to wake her. Matron tells her she has been searching all over the hospital looking for her. Abby apologizes for falling asleep on the job. Matron smiles and tells her she deserves it. She goes on to say that Mr. Grant told her what a great job Abby did in the OR today. She tells Abby that everyone is proud of her and she deserves to leave a little early today. Abby looks at the clock and sees that it is 5:30. She lets out a little chuckle and Matron helps her from the floor.

She walks back to the portal slowly because she is so tired. By the time she gets into her house it is 1:30 in the morning. She changes her clothes and is about to hop into bed when her phone rings. While debating with herself whether to answer or not the machine picks up the call. It is Susan her supervisor. There was a night club shooting and they need Abby at the hospital as soon as possible. Abby looks in the mirror and shakes her head. She gets dressed and is out the door within a few minutes. On the way to the hospital she stops and picks up a large coffee.

After pulling into a parking space Abby sits in her car for a few minutes to finish her coffee. When the cup is empty she slowly exits her car. Still a little groggy from working in 1939.

As soon as she enters the hospital Abby goes right to the OR and begins her shift of non-stop surgeries until the crises is over. After washing up Abby looks at the clock.

3:00 pm is the time and Abby is totally drained. Susan approaches her and as Abby turns to talk to her Susan can see that Abby is exhausted.

"Go home and get some rest. Tomorrow looks to be a light schedule." Susan says and she pats Abby on the back. "Nice work today. We really were impressed with your work. Now go!"

Abby gives Susan a slight grin and slowly walks to her car. She enters her home and flops down on her bed not even bothering to undress. In less than a minute she is sound asleep.

Chapter 23

August 29, 2019.

Dave kisses Emily goodbye as he heads over to Abby's for yard work and some repair work. Being so busy with two hospital jobs, she has no time to devote to keeping her house under control. She called Dave and asked him if he wouldn't mind helping her out. He agrees and this is the first day he is able to help her. As he walks into the kitchen, he sees the sink full of dishes and coffee spilled on the counter. The coffee maker needs to be cleaned and there is something in the microwave that she forgot. He starts on the coffee maker and brews himself a pot. After sitting and sipping his coffee, he finishes cleaning the kitchen. He starts the laundry and even replaces the towels and bed linens.

While cleaning the bathroom he pauses, looks in the mirror and says, "I might make someone a good wife someday." Then he laughs and says, "Better to be a good husband to Emily." When the last of the laundry is dry and folded, Dave looks at the time. He has spent over four hours working on Abby's house. The last of his projects is to readjust the garage door. Somehow the hinges loosened, and the door is very hard to close. It takes him about an hour to fix the door, and as soon as he is finished, Abby appears at the door gently tapping on the glass. Dave smiles at her and opens the door, showing her how easy it is to open and close now. They have a nice pleasant chat over a cup of coffee, and Abby asks Dave if he has gone through the portal lately. He tells her he hasn't but thinks about going back to Hollywood and picking up some more silver coins. The problem with that is getting into the studio after he exits into the street. Abby tells him it isn't worth the time and effort and Dave reluctantly agrees. They sit and chat for about twenty more minutes when Dave tells Abby he really needs to get going. As he is about to go out the door, she tells him to forget about Hollywood; but if he really wants to travel, go to London in 1939. He smiles and closes the door as he leaves.

Abby finishes her coffee and sits down with her notebook. She has been a little lax in her writing about what has been happening, and she devotes a good hour to writing all about what she has been doing in 1939 and in 2019. After rereading her notes, she puts the pen and notebook down and drifts off to sleep.

August 30, 2019.

Abby calls Dave and asks if he can come over tomorrow. She is having trouble with her kitchen sink. The drain seems to be clogged again. She has called him multiple times about this same issue. He keeps telling her not to dump the coffee grounds down the drain, but for some reason she hasn't listened to him.

August 31, 2019

Dave arrives early Saturday morning to fix the drain.

It only takes him about ten minutes to clear the problem with him berating Abby about the coffee grounds the entire time he is working. She is standing behind him saying, "Blah, blah, blah, blah, blah," and then laughing. As he closes the cabinet and stands up, the coffee maker chimes to signal the pot is ready. Abby makes them each a cup, and they sit down at the table to sip. She asks him what his plans are for the rest of the day and he says he has none. Emily is taking the kids shopping for new clothes, and he has no interest in spending the day in the mall shopping. Abby laughs and says she doesn't understand. Shopping for children's clothes sounds like so much fun. Dave rolls his eyes and tells her she should join them and find out how much fun it is. They both stop talking and just sip their coffee as they stare into space.

After a long stretch of silence, Abby asks Dave if he would like to go through the portal. She has the day off and needs to go to 1939 and do something. Her something is bringing Douglas some racing results. Dave thinks for a moment and says, "Why not."

While Abby is getting ready, Dave cleans the coffee cups. He shouts to Abby that she needs a maid, and she shouts back that she doesn't need one because she has him as her slave. She pokes her head into the kitchen (smiling and batting her eyes) telling him she has been waiting for him for hours. He shakes his head and slowly walks into the garage.

Dave is wearing blue jeans and a plain white dirty T-shirt, so he figures he should be able to blend in. As long as no one examines his boots to carefully, he feels safe enough. Abby asks him why he isn't changing into something more period appropriate, and he tells her he is feeling lazy and doesn't feel like changing.

They wander out of the warehouse and onto the pavement, walking to the corner where they find the entrance to the East End Pub. Dave has been past this entrance many times but for some odd reason never gone inside. Abby goes into the pub leaving Dave outside. After standing outside the entrance to the pub for a few minutes, Dave decides to go inside. He walks up to the bar and asks for a lager. He stops himself and realizes he has no wallet or early 1900s British currency. The pretty young barmaid, who looks amazingly like his own wife Emily (when she was in her early twenties) smiles at him and says. "Haven't seen you round here before?"

"No," he says, "I just arrived. I'm from (he pauses) out of town. I ordered the lager before I realized I haven't any money. I'm sorry."

The barmaid winks at Dave, smiles and says. "That's all right, catch me up next time." As he thanks her for the lager, Douglas walks up to the two of them.

"What's your business in here, young man? And why aren't you in a uniform," Douglas asks him.

"I am an American," Dave answers, and before he could say another word he sees his reflection in the mirror. He appears to be in his early twenties. When he was in Abby's garage, he was in his middle forties. He is mesmerized by his youthful appearance. So much so that he is speechless. Douglas walks away mumbling "I got my eyes on you, son." Douglas goes to the back where Abby is sitting at a table. He joins Abby; and from where they are sitting they cannot see Dave and Emilie. Abby didn't see Dave enter the pub, and Dave doesn't see Abby sitting in the back.

The barmaid smiles. "We don't get many Yanks in here. In fact, I think you might be the first one." The pub is slow at this time, and the barmaid stands nearby looking at and smiling at Dave. Dave, still staring at his reflection, doesn't notice the police constable walk up behind him. "The usual, Bobby?" the barmaid calls out.

The officer replies. "Don't mind if I do." Bobby, the police officer, turns to Dave, and says. "Hello there. I am officer Robert Doyle of the Metropolitan Police Force. And who might you be?"

"Day uh um Dave. My name is Dave." Dave stumbles with his words.

"Are you here on business or pleasure, son?" Bobby asks him.

"Um uh um p pleasure, b b business?" Dave responds (still stumbling with his words). Without taking his gaze from the mirror.

"Not sure, then are you?" Bobby asks.
Dave doesn't answer, but slowly turns to face the man asking him the questions.

Dave smiles and gives a slight laugh. "Bobby the Bobby, that's funny." Dave says.

"Gee, never heard that one before." Bobby answers back. The officer looks a little like Reginald Deadman from the "Goodnight Sweetheart" television series. The barmaid looks a little like Phoebe, but more like Dave's wife Emily, and the Barman looks like Phoebe's dad Eric. Dave reaches his hand out to shake Bobby's hand, and Bobby gives him a jolly good hand pump. Dave turns his gaze to the barmaid.

"My name is Dave, and you are?"

"Emilie with an ie," replies the barmaid.

Dave takes his drink, and sits at the table in the back of the pub where Abby and Douglas were sitting. Abby went to the ladie's room, and Douglas went back behind the bar. There is a heated darts game going on, and news of the possibility of war is on the wireless. The calendar next to the dart board is on August 1939. Dave, not seeing Abby, finishes his lager in one big gulp and says he will be back soon as he walks out the door onto the pavement. He is standing looking down the street to see if he can see Abby, but he sees no sign of her.

Emilie comes out of the pub and smiles at Dave.

"Please come back soon," she says as she slowly goes back inside. No sooner does she disappear than Abby comes through the door. She sees Dave standing and thinks he has been there the entire time she was inside. She asks Dave if he wants to go inside for a drink, but he tells her he just came out. He was inside chatting with Emilie and didn't see her inside. Abby just shrugs, and the two of them wander around for a couple of hours.

Back through the portal, Dave says goodbye to Abby and drives off thinking about Emilie. Abby goes into her house sits on her father's chair and writes all about today's trip through the portal.

THE END